I0578715

DESERT SHAMAN

WHISKEY WITCHES ANCIENTS BOOK 1

F.J. BLOODING

This is a work of fiction. All the characters, organizations, and events within this book are products of the author's imagination or are used fictitiously. Any resemblance to business establishments, actual persons, or events is entirely coincidental. The publisher does not have any control over and does not assume any responsibility for author or third-party websites or their content.

Copyright © 2017 Frankie Blooding / Whistling Book Press
All rights reserved.
Per the U.S. Copyright Act of 1976, no part of this publication may be reproduced, scanned, or distributed in any form without written permission from the publisher. Please only purchase authorized editions.

Printed in the United States of America

Published by Whistling Book Press
Whistling Book Press

Alaska
Visit our web site at:

www.whistlingbookpress.com

ALSO BY F.J. BLOODING

Whiskey Witches Universe

Whiskey Witches

Whiskey Witches

Blood Moon Magick

Barrel of Whiskey

Witches of the West

Whiskey Witches: Ancients

Desert Shaman

Big Bad Djinn

Lizard Wizard

Whiskey on the Rocks

Double-Double Demon Trouble

Mirror, Mirror Demon Rubble

Dead Demon Die

Whiskey Witches: Para Wars

Whiskey Storm

London Bridge Down

Midnight Whiskey

International Team of Mystery

Slipping on Karma Peels

Pre-order now at: https://www.fjblooding.com/preorder

Other Books in the Whiskey-Verse

Shifting Heart Romances

by Hattie Hunt & F.J. Blooding

Bear Moon

Grizzly Attraction

Here's the reading order to make it even easier to catch up!

https://www.fjblooding.com/reading-order

Other Books by F.J. Blooding

Devices of War Trilogy

Fall of Sky City

Sky Games

Whispers of the Skyborne

Discover more, sign up for updates and gifts, and join the forum discussions at www.fjblooding.com.

WHISKEY MAGICK & MENTAL HEALTH

SIGN UP TO learn more about our books and receive this free e-zine about Whiskey Magick and Mental Health.
https://www.fjblooding.com/books-lp

*To my amazing husband.
We've been through a lot.
We're still alive. How about that?*

ONE

"HEADS UP," Leslie called from the stove.

Paige dutifully looked up in time to snatch a jar of peanut butter out of the air. Her reflexes were getting fast. She attributed that to the fact that she was now chasing after a young toddler in her free time who was doing his best to cram all the hot dog pieces into his mouth at the same time.

"Are you chewing?" she asked Bobby, setting the jar down on the table.

He mumbled a "uh-huh" and shoved another cut into his bulging cheeks.

Well, if he was breathing, he was wasn't dying. Right? She turned to her sister and gestured to the peanut butter. "What's up?"

Leslie took a partial loaf of bread and lobbed it from the large open kitchen to the wide yet somehow still cramped dining room. "You haven't eaten all day."

"Oh." Paige caught the bread before slices tumbled out the open bag. Her sister was good at looking out for her, which was nice. Paige hadn't quite realized just how "hard working" she was until she'd moved in with her family.

Alma lumbered in with a heavy sigh, her grey hair a frizzled mess like always. "What in the world are you on about now?"

It seemed like Alma—the grandmother who'd raised both Leslie and Paige—was always asking her that. But in the past several months, Paige had been doing a lot less of her normal stuff—being a detective—and a lot more other stuff. That other stuff *should* have included managing a team of paranormal investigators, but that wasn't what took *most* of her time.

No, that was going around from one pack to another, from one paranormal group to another, and trying to bring them under one banner.

But at that *very* moment, she was reviewing the Red Star Division's budget. They *had* one. Barely. And at some point, they were going to need more. They needed office equipment and supplies. Most of what they had in that building had come from her personal cash stash, which wasn't very big to begin with. Especially not with a growing toddler and a fashion tween.

But, luckily, Bobby was being raised in a big family and so he got a lot of hand me downs. That and Alma *loved* to garage sale. Anything they needed, she'd find for fifty cents on a Friday afternoon.

Oh, the things she was learning about her family.

Alma took the bread back to the toaster to make Paige her favorite, peanut butter toast with the peanut butter melted into the bread.

Paige really did love that woman.

"What's the business in Montana?" Alma asked,

plunking the bread down and opening the silverware drawer with a jerk.

"Grandma," Leslie cried, putting the finishing touches on her coffee mix drink. "I gave it to her so she could make it."

"And one day you'll figure out that some people just need a little help." Alma pushed Leslie away like a fly. "Your sister's one of 'em."

"I *can* make my own," Paige said, feeling guilty. But if she had a choice between plowing through work or taking a break to wait on a toaster, she was going to work.

Bobby choked on his hotdogs.

Paige got up to assist with a sigh. One day, that little boy would become a man. She shoved a finger in his mouth and pulled out slobbery hotdog pieces. But back to the subject, she'd been called to Montana to try and get a group of hedge witches to join the Elder Council. Chuck had even considered the possibility of bringing them into his pack, which Paige found a little odd. She didn't understand what either wanted with this many paranormals. "Montana was a bust. Everyone hid from me the entire time."

"What *are* you trying to do?" Leslie asked, bringing over her journal and her coffee concoction.

"I wish I knew." Because it felt like Paige was a pawn in some really big game and she didn't know all the rules. She fished most of the hot dog out of Bobby's mouth and gave the toddler a frank look. "Chew."

He gasped for air, but nodded, his blue eyes narrowed with determination.

"You've gotta know something," Leslie muttered as she threw her book open. It was tabbed with sticky notes and torn pieces of paper taped randomly.

Paige's brain hurt trying to make sense of her chaos. "What are *you* up to?"

Leslie looked up at her with one narrowed eye and a look of excitement. "I've got an idea for a new soap."

"Neat." And it was. Paige knew nothing about soaps or how to use them—for spells. She knew how to wash her hands—but Leslie had opened a soap shop and she was doing great. "What does—"

"No," Leslie said, slamming her hands on the table. "Enough with the secrets. Tell us already."

Bobby flailed his hands against his table. "Tell! Tell! Te —" He choked on another hotdog.

Paige watched him but he got it worked out. "The only thing I know is that Chuck thinks there's something big on the horizon and he's gathering as many players as he can."

"He ain't wrong." Alma came to the table and plunked down the toast and a knife.

Paige had scant time to get the peanut butter on before the toast cooled too much, so she went to work slathering. "I know that Sven's doing something." He was a demon slash angel slash sorcerer slash serial killer she hadn't been able to hunt down and lock away yet. He'd escaped her in Louisiana and again in Colorado. But as far as "big things" on the horizon went, that was the only thing she could see.

And they didn't *need* packs and they didn't *need* other paranormal communities. She just needed to do her job and catch him.

"Will he *ever* go away? But Chuck. You must have a theory," Leslie said, letting her head fall back. "Why does everything have to be so secretive with you?"

"It's not secretive. It's just not—there's nothing to tell." Though, there *were* secrets. She couldn't discuss cases or special operations. She was privy to information she couldn't share. "I get the feeling that something more political is happening with the Elder Council. What do we even know about them?"

Leslie raised her eyebrows and shook her head.

Paige knew they were a council of powerful members who were trying to create laws and regulations for the paranormal communities. That *could be* good, but Paige didn't get the best feeling from them. She didn't think they were *evil*. She just didn't think they were really good.

She screwed the lid of the peanut butter back on, pleased with herself. It was melting into her toast nicely.

"You think they're planning to tak—"

Leslie was interrupted by Paige's phone.

Of course. This, also, had become the new normal of her life. She was constantly on call. She never got a night off. She pulled her phone out of her back pocket and looked at the screen. "Work."

Leslie rolled her eyes and went back to her notes.

Alma got up and went to Bobby, taking the hot dog pieces away from him.

"Hey, Paige," Rainbow said over the phone, her tone hesitant. "I know—"

She was drowned out by Bobby's screams of outrage over having lost his hotdog.

"Grandma, would you—"

"He's going to turn into a brat," Alma growled, crumpling the paper towel with the hotdog pieces in one hand and keeping them out of Paige's reach.

"I'm trying to work," Paige said, frustrated. She managed to free one hotdog piece and gave it to her toddler.

He chirped happily and shoved it in his mouth.

"Sorry, Bow," Paige said, leaving the dining room and

heading into the furniture-crowded living room. "I didn't catch any of that."

"We got a new case and I need you," Rainbow shouted quickly.

Which was a new record for her. Rainbow could talk and talk and talk and never get to the point. "Michelle can't handle it?"

"She's on her own case."

"Dexx?"

"He's—" Rainbow stopped. Paige could almost see her turning in her chair, looking for him. "Actually, I have no idea where he is."

Dexx was a great hunter but turning him into a paranormal law enforcement officer was proving difficult. "I'll be right there."

"Hey, thanks!"

Paige hung up before Rainbow could slam her with a thousand and one other questions. "Grandma," she called, coming back into the dining room.

Bobby and Alma were fighting over hotdogs. Bobby was glowing with a golden light as he tried to use his magick to get his treat.

Alma threw up some magick of her own. It was going to be a fight over an afternoon snack. Geez.

"Bobby," Paige barked.

The golden light disappeared as he looked balefully up at her with tears in his blue eyes.

Paige hated that look. She walked over to Alma who had also put her magick away and took the hotdogs. She opened the paper towel and focused on her son. "One." She set them down as she counted. "Two. In your mouth. Chew Swallow." She gave him a hard mom-look. "One. Two. That's it. Then chew."

"Two. Two," he said forcefully, and shoved the two offered pieces in his mouth, making a big show of chewing.

With the hotdog bomb defused, Paige turned to Alma. "Work called. They need me."

"Not surprised." Alma held out her hand. "One," She grumbled. "Two." She *really* didn't look pleased.

"You're teaching him to think, Grandma. He's a *baby*." She handed off the treasure and went to collect her work stuff.

"He *could* be forever!"

Paige rolled her eyes so hard they hurt as she headed for the door.

The drive to the precinct didn't take too long. At one of the lights, she picked up her phone and texted Dexx. *Where are you?*

By the time she parked her silver sedan in the parking lot at Red Star, she had a reply. *On stakeout. Bring me a sandwich.*

She decided to ignore that last part. *Who are you investigating?*

The three dots appeared, showing he was working on his reply, but she wasn't going to sit around and wait. She got out of the car, gathered her stuff and headed toward the door, waiting for the vibration to alert her to his message.

Oliver. Don't trust him. Bring sandwich. [*sandwich emoji*]

Paige and the team had managed to bring down Oliver Eastwood's mother just a few months prior. She was a blood witch, which, technically, wasn't bad. Except she was two hundred years old and had managed to use her blood magick to sacrifice people and extend her life. Olly was Paige's half-brother and her brother-in-law in a weird twist of events that still made Paige's eyebrow twitch as she heard a banjo in the back of her mind. Her biological father had really been intent on sowing his seed through the witch lines, trying to make a more powerful witch.

It certainly looked like he'd succeeded with Paige.

She paused at the door and texted, *Play it by the book. I'm not kidding.*

The dots didn't appear, but his icon did, showing he'd at least gotten the message.

She finally made it into the bullpen. She couldn't help the smile on her face. She'd been working in police bullpens for over a decade. They were cold and severe. It didn't matter how the desks were arranged. A civilian walked into the bullpen and your stomach dropped.

That wasn't what Paige had wanted the reaction to *her* bullpen to be. She wanted people to realize this place was different, that her team was different, and that it wasn't a bad thing to be there. So, she'd used her magick and had made the walls separating each desk a line of plants with something significant for each person who worked in each space.

Rainbow was a rusalka, so she was tied to water. In her cubical, Paige had set up a water feature, but made sure to keep it away from all electronic devices. Rainbow was a great investigator, but she was also a mild klutz.

Her phone buzzed as she walked past Rainbow's cubicle. "Dropping off my stuff."

Rainbow looked up. She'd pulled her afro back in a series of small pom-tails? Paige didn't know how else to describe it. She wasn't certain she'd know how to maintain hair as amazing as Rainbow's, but she missed the fun and free-loving afro Rainbow normally sported.

Rainbow's eyes lit up and she stood, knocking something over on the desk behind her, which fell into something else, which landed onto something else. Glass cracked.

Paige raised her eyebrows. "I'll give you a minute."

Rainbow frowned and went to work on cleaning up the chaos. "It's okay."

Paige wasn't certain *what* was "okay," but she kept walking.

The phone buzzed several more times.

Paige shook her head and dumped her bag and jacket on the chair opposite her desk, looking out across the bullpen again through the windows. Sure enough, no one was around.

As the person who managed this office, she should have a better idea of where her people were.

Tarik, their djinn, was off with Quinn, their siren, on investigation in Portland. Paige didn't *want* them in Portland *doing* anything because they had zero jurisdiction there. Her boss was the local sheriff. There were there for information only.

Except that there *was* demon activity going on over there and Paige needed information. She had a face that was hard to hide in the demon world, being the demon summoner and all. She just hoped Tarik and Quinn were keeping their noses out of too much trouble.

Michelle was investigating a case Sheriff Tuck had handed them the day before, a series of thefts that didn't make sense by human standards. So, something had to be going on.

Dexx was investigating someone who didn't *need* to be investigated. She was going to have to talk to him about how budgets and money worked.

She picked up her phone as it vibrated three more times.

It was a string of sandwich emojis and a cucumber she was pretty sure he'd meant to be a pickle. He loved pickles, but hated cucumbers. She smiled and sent him a poop emoji.

Rainbow burst in with a small case file and a mess of papers.

Seeing the disorganization made Paige wince in pain, but it worked for Rainbow. Paige didn't understand how.

Her phone vibrated and a sad face emoji flitted to the top of her lock screen.

Paige chortled inside and put her phone face down on her desk. "What's up?"

"A bad, bad man." Rainbow set down the file, picked it up, set it down, and picked it back up again. "I—" She flicked her gaze to the ceiling and then back to Paige again. "You're going to say no."

"Why?"

"Because, um." Rainbow narrowed her eyes and licked her lips. "It's...personal?"

Rainbow was what most *real* detectives would call an amateur. She had no training, but she had a natural inclination. So that meant there were a lot of things she didn't know. Which made things difficult for Paige because she'd been the one who'd had to teach the rusalka all these rules. Simple things like don't touch or contaminate evidence. Or don't get messed up in an investigation you're personally tied to.

"Which is why I wanted to give it to you."

Oh, great. Paige gestured to the chair that didn't have her stuff in it and sat down. "Convince me."

Rainbow perched on the edge of the seat and launched into a big explanation about how she'd broken up with her girlfriend—which Paige had known. She'd taken it really hard—and how her girlfriend had already moved on with this new guy—which *wasn't* weird because she was bi? Paige was willing to accept people for who they were, but a few things were hard for her to wrap her head around.

But the "currents" had been talking to Rainbow quite a bit lately and had been telling her that this guy was a "bad man" and that she needed to dig into him a bit more. Rainbow didn't know *what* was wrong about this guy, only that he was bad and that her ex-girlfriend might be in danger.

To be fair, water was a terrible communicator, speaking in visions and emotions that weren't super clear all the time.

"I've told you about building walls between you and the currents," Paige said, ignoring her vibrating phone. Sometimes she wished she could put it on do-not-disturb, but someone with real issues might need her instead of her annoying boyfriend.

"I know. I know." Rainbow's shoulders drooped. "But —" She licked her lips, her palms up on her stack of papers. "You know how you're listening to music and it's great and it makes you feel good and then you turn on the really good headphones that block out sound and you can't hear it anymore?"

Paige didn't *have* a set of headphones *that* good. "I'm a mom. I'm always broke."

"Oh, well, it's great. But you can't hear the music anymore."

"That's...kind of the point." Paige's phone buzzed again.

"Well, that music is the juice of my soul. I *need* to hear it."

"Oh." Paige leaned back in her chair and grabbed her phone to tell Dexx to stop. "Okay. Leave it on my desk and

I'll look. Tell the currents you've got someone working on it."

Rainbow leapt to her feet with a beaming grin. "Thanks, boss." She set the stack on Paige's desk, picked it back up, searching for a better place.

Paige pointed to a relatively blank space.

With another radiating smile, Rainbow set it down and hopped toward the door.

"Work on one of the cases Tuck brought us," Paige called after Rainbow and then muttered to herself, "Someone needs to actually earn their keep around here." She looked at the phone, expecting more emojis and there *were* some. Several in fact.

But there were also several messages from Chuck, the regional high alpha. The last one left no room for argument.

Get over here. Elder sanctuary. Now. A situation has come up.

Crap. Rainbow's case was just going to have to wait.

TWO

PAIGE GRABBED her bag and jacket and headed for the car. She passed Rainbow's desk and stopped. "Chuck called."

Rainbow frowned up at her. "How many bosses do you have?"

Paige sighed. "Just the two. I wish they'd coordinate."

"My case?"

"Crap." Paige moved to go retrieve it from her desk.

Rainbow jumped up instead and brought it to her in a quick jaunt.

Paige opened her bag and shoved it inside. "We really need to work on your organization next."

"Sure thing, boss."

"And be sure to work on the cases Tuck gave us. And if you see Michelle, remind her what it means to earn a paycheck. She'll know what I mean."

Rainbow frowned but swung her clasped hands in a gung-ho gesture. "Okay."

She was still at her desk not working on the cases,

though. So, Paige gave her a frank look and winced significantly.

Rainbow didn't take the hint for a long moment, then understanding dawned. Her mouth came open and she pointed a finger as she leapt—the woman had to be part gazelle—toward the stack on the spare desk. "I was looking for a gift for Ethel."

Ethel was their lab tech the basement. "For what?"

"She's getting a new couch. It arrives in three days."

"You don't—" Well, the rest of the world might not give presents for a new couch, but Rainbow used any occasion to give people thoughtful gifts. "On your own time, Bow."

"Right." Rainbow clutched a handful of files to her chest and shot Paige a toothy smile that read something like, "Isn't it time you left yet because I hear two-day shipping calling me."

Paige released a long breath and headed for her car more frustrated now than she had been a moment before.

Her phone vibrated again. It was Dexx. *Haven't killed him. Deserve reward.*

She needed him to stop. *Chuck called. Headed out.*

Silence.

Paige really needed to make better boundaries when it came to Chuck and his packs and the Elder Council and their politics. She was a detective and a powerful witch. But she was a detective, running her first-ever paranormal investigation team. This was the dream she'd never realized she'd had.

The elders didn't seem to understand little things like making time to raise kids or earn a paycheck, and Chuck didn't understand things like loyalty to something other than his pack.

Technically, she was a part of it because she housed a

shifter spirit, but she hadn't been bitten, so she wasn't... whatever happened when a witch was bitten by a shifter. Would she have lost her magick?

But Cawli, her spirit animal, did help her keep the door to Hell that had been branded into her bones shut, and for that she was eternally grateful.

Grateful enough to answer the call to a regional high alpha who wasn't *really* her alpha.

But after taking down Merry Eastwood who had once reigned magickal witchy terror over this area, she had inadvertently brought the witches back into the elder council fold of paranormal law. Something she'd *been* glad about.

Except for some reason she was now the lead person to deal with anything paranormal for them. She almost felt like their personal security detail. What had they done before her, she wanted to know.

Just a couple of days ago, Paige'd spent a week in Portland dealing with a demon problem. The elder council had ordered her out there for that.

But Paige had a suspicion that was less their problem and more hers. Sven was like this itch in the back of her mind she couldn't get rid of. He was so slippery and extremely calculating. She didn't know if she was smart enough to bring him in on her own.

Powerful enough? Probably, especially now that she had her shifter spirit animal keeping Sven's door to Hell wedged closed.

But what was he doing with demons? That was the only explanation for the rise in numbers she could think of. What was he planning?

And would she ever be enough to take him down and bring him to justice? It bothered her that a serial killer was still on the loose because she didn't know how to bring him down. She should be focusing on *that* and not on whatever errand her regional high alpha was going to send her on.

How had she been talked into this elder gig again?

The ride out of town and to the elder property wasn't that far by Colorado standards where "the other side of town" was over an hour away, but it gave her plenty of time to think. The highway wound up the mountain for several miles. She turned onto a small, blacktop road before she crested the top.

The tall trees unwove, opening a scene in front of her that didn't seem as though it belonged on planet Earth.

Whenever she thought of the elders, she always pictured square buildings and rigid rules. She didn't picture this level of opulence.

The elder "sanctuary" looked like a multi-million-dollar mansion that she would only see in magazines. It was tall, wide, and had turrets. She wasn't kidding. It looked like a frelling castle.

The trees rewove behind her closing off the road again.

She parked her car in the circular drive in front of the wide dark hardwood door, cut the engine to her silver Mazda and got out, leaving her bag there. The front door opened before she even managed to make it up to the stone steps.

The man that she had taken to calling Bart—she still didn't know his name because he never gave it—smiled at her. He was tall with gray hair and aging skin, and he always wore a black suit. He was the quintessential butler. "Good day, Miss Whiskey."

"Morning, Bart." She stepped through the doorway, walking past him.

He winced at the name. But it was his own damned fault. She'd asked. He hadn't given it. She understood wanting to keep some semblance of privacy, especially if he didn't trust her. However, if he wanted her to call him by something he liked better, he was going to have to share it. Maybe she should pull a Dexx and find a more irritating name for him.

Bart showed her to the library with a forced smile and a slight bow and then disappeared.

Paige didn't mind the library. It smelled like old books and, while she didn't recognize most of the titles, she did enjoy running her fingers along the spines and imagining what some of the mysteries might be in those massive volumes. In that moment, it was almost as if she could read via osmosis. However, when she stepped into the large room this time, she was met by Chuck.

It was a rare thing for Chuck to be involved in elder business. That alone should have raised her alert level, but in her defense, she had a lot on her plate. She had a para-normal unit that didn't know how to follow rules, she had a budget she didn't know how to manage, and a toddler who was set on killing himself with food.

But as soon as she saw him, she realized something big was afoot.

He rose from one of the leather chairs just as a door closed at the back of the room.

Had she interrupted a meeting?

Chuck had a Mediterranean movie-star look to him, with his curly dark hair and his bright blue eyes. He smiled and met her halfway clasping her hand in both of his. "Have a seat," he said in his slight accent she still couldn't place, even after knowing him for over a year.

This didn't sound good. "What's going on? I've got a few other things I need to take care of, so I'm hoping this is big and not 'we need the trash taken out.'"

"No." Chuck sank into one of the chairs, the leather creaking with his weight. "This particular situation requires your attention."

She really didn't want to hear it. In that moment, all her frustration at being pulled in so many different directions while not being able to focus on the things that mattered to her boiled to the surface. "What about my kids? How am I supposed to be a mother when I'm never home?"

Chuck didn't say anything. He just studied her as she sat opposite him.

Which was something he did, listen. That wasn't necessarily a bad thing. However, in situations like this, she didn't need him to *listen*. She needed him to *do*. "In the past several months, I haven't seen my kids more than a few days. I just got my daughter back, and Dexx spends more time with her more than I do. He's basically raising my daughter right now. So, why the hell did I even fight to get her back when I can't spend any time with her?"

Chuck rested his elbows on the arms of the chair and steepled his fingers. "I do not know what to say to that."

Huh. He didn't know what to say to that. Again, that was very helpful. "I have a brand-new baby boy. A brand-new baby boy who's walking now and guess who missed his first steps."

Chuck winced.

"Yeah. Me. His supposed mother. I've missed his first steps. I've missed his first words. What else am I going to miss? Oh, that's right. Everything because I'm so damned important? I'm not. I'm not the *most powerful witch* in the area." Was she? With Merry Eastwood locked up, who filled *that* spot now? "I'm not a shifter. I'm not...*anyone* except a failing investigative—" What *was* her title? "—manager and a failing mother."

Chuck pressed a fingertip into his chin, "How is the pregnancy? Have you noticed anything unusual?"

Paige frowned at him, shocked into silence. She was keeping that on the hush-hush. How the hell had he known?

He quirked his lips with the affirmation of her silence. "I have been around many pregnant female shifters. There are changes. Smells. Moods." He leaned forward. "Sex drive."

How the hell had he figured *that* out? His nose was one thing? Paige had discovered she couldn't keep *anything* hidden from a shifter nose. But how'd he know about her sex drive?

He sat back. "Pheromones. When you release them into a pack, it is called going into heat. All of the males notice."

Oh great. Just one more reason why she wasn't overly thrilled with the possibility of staying around more shifters. She certainly hoped the next mission didn't involve another pack.

"I have concerns."

She settled back in her chair, glancing at the door in the back. "I don't necessarily believe I want to have this conversation here."

"It's the safest place in the area to have a conversation just like this."

What was that supposed to mean? Were there prying eyes and ears everywhere else? "Okay."

"You are very powerful witch."

"I'm glad you noticed." That wasn't the *only* thing getting bigger. So were her reflexes and her senses. She ignored a lot of it because she didn't want to recognize that her sight was getting *better* instead of worse, and she certainly didn't want to develop a better sense of smell.

Mostly, she didn't want to admit what *might* be going on with her.

She was pregnant for the first time since Leah who was now a tween and a lot had happened with her magick since then. Her powers had been locked away and then had been ripped open more powerful than ever. She'd had a demon door installed in her breastbone and ribs. She'd invited a shifter spirit to share her meatsuit.

And she was growing a child who would be a powerful witch.

Or a powerful shifter because her or his father was one of the strongest shifters in the area. A moron at times, but still a very powerful shifter.

Or maybe her child would be both shifter and witch.

What would that look like?

But moreover, her power was growing. Sometimes explosively. Small things were big. She would use magick without even thinking about it. Her radio in her car no longer worked because she'd turned up the volume using her magick, then had freaked out about it and had over-reacted.

Was this just the pregnancy? Or would some of this power stay?

Who would keep her in check if she got too big? All she had to do was to look at Merry Eastwood. She'd been the most powerful witch in the area, and she'd gone dark. Would Paige? After all she'd seen and all she'd done? Would *she* go dark?

Alma had always been the one to keep her in check before. Alma was the most powerful kitchen witch Paige knew, but...

Paige had even outgrown her since even *before* the pregnancy.

Chuck watched her internal conversation, waiting for it to end. He raised his chin and his eyebrows before dropping both. "You are a witch and you have a shifter spirit inside you."

"You just received the Crown of Obviousness."

He went still, piercing her with the power of his alpha gaze.

Cawli stirred in the back of Paige's mind. The power of the alpha's gaze held her almost in thrall. When Chuck had her like this, she couldn't disobey. She hated it when he did it, but it oddly made her feel comforted. *He* had the power to keep her in check. She just had to make sure she didn't outgrow *him*.

He raised a dark eyebrow. "You are a shifter-witch."

"Except I can't shift." Something she didn't understand. But Cawli was insistent it wasn't possible and she hadn't challenge it. She was already too strong for her own good.

Chuck's eye twitched.

That was almost the confirmation she needed. She'd suspected that he and Cawli had been lying to her.

When they'd moved to Oregon, they'd been attacked by hyenas. She was almost certain she'd started to shift in that battle. She couldn't say for sure, but it had felt like it. She'd almost felt her bones morphing. However, so many other things that happened that day. She'd nearly killed another shifter by using her magic. That had terrified her. She hadn't even wanted to consider the implication that she could do that *and* shift.

But why would Chuck and Cawli tell her she couldn't? Why would *they* lie to her? She understood why *she* would lie to herself.

Cawli rumbled in the back of her mind, shifting his soul weight uncomfortably in the back of her existence.

"Are you like your sister?"

Paige didn't understand what Chuck was asking. She shook her head.

"Are you able to use the gifts of your unborn child?"

She hadn't even thought of that. Frankly, she'd forgotten about it. "I doubt it. I don't remember raising the dead a single time when I was pregnant with Leah."

Chuck nodded, his expression relaxing minutely. "You have to be very careful, Paige."

He'd said her name, which meant things were serious, but her only response was no shit.

Because...if she was carrying a child who *could potentially* be a shifter-witch as he'd called it and she *wasn't* using her baby's abilities like Leslie had been able to—oh, crap! How had she *forgotten* the stories of Alma and Tru having to hide from Leslie when she'd been pregnant with Kamden the telepath?

But if Paige's powers were growing and her senses were getting stronger, did that mean *she* was a shifter-witch? She hadn't been bitten. So, she wasn't a *real* shifter. Real shifters had to be bitten.

"There has been a shift in power." Chuck sat up straighter in his chair. "Something has happened and we do not know what it is. The power of our pack has grown. I do not know why. I fear that it has to do with your child or with you yourself."

She frowned. "I don't understand."

He looked away as if trying to form his words. "Dexx is a very powerful alpha."

Well, that's what everybody said. He wasn't particularly smart. However, she still loved him.

"In order for him to remain in control of himself, he needs a pack big enough to relieve some of his power."

"Like paper towels after a spill?" Paige was *trying* to understand what he was saying.

Chuck took a deep breath. "This is something that I did not take into consideration when we accepted you into the pack."

What was he talking about?

"Bringing the Whiskeys *and* Dexx into my region has unbalanced our power—my power. You should be reli—you should be *my* paper towel, but instead I am yours."

She appreciated the fact he'd used her reference. "Because I'm getting more powerful." This didn't bode well. They'd moved to Oregon knowing Chuck would be there to assist them. While she'd fought it at first, Chuck had become an instrumental part of Paige's team. She relied on him now.

Would the kids be kicked out of school if she got kicked out of the pack? They were finally making friends and were fitting in for probably the first time since any of them could remember and this was coming from the viewpoint that they were witches in a shifter community that feared witches. So, that said a lot.

"There is a large, powerful regional pack in Utah," Chuck said.

"Okay?" Did they have answers?

Chuck took in a deep breath. "They are threatening to leave the folds of the Elder Council."

Which the elders didn't want for their own reason. She couldn't tell if it was a power trip or if the elders sincerely cared. They acted as a protective government, but, like all governments and religious bodies that held power, there was that threat of the power-hungry. And Paige couldn't determine if that threat legitimately existed there or not.

"Their reason for leaving is because of you."

"Because of my family or because of me?" But she also realized the bigger issue. It was less that the elders were upset about the pack leaving and more that Chuck *needed* them to stay if she and Dexx were going to remain in the regional pack. If Utah left, Dexx and Paige might have to as well.

Chuck watched the internal conversation without adding to it. He was one of the few people who almost seemed to hear or watch it. "You."

Crap. She'd faced this in Kansas, too. It had been a big deal until everyone there got to know her, and then it all fizzled out. It had felt a little like de-energizing a nuke with a kitten. Lots of drama, then nothing. "Okay. So, why do I care? I don't. The Elder Council can pound sand." Not really, but she needed to make a stand somewhere.

"The Elder Council is tied to my pack and we to them." Chuck shook his head slightly, his expression stating it had seemed like a good idea at the time, but that he was now wondering if the benefits outweighed the price.

Well, there went that. "I guess I can kiss a few babies and smooth things over."

Chuck drummed his thumb on his knee. "They want to put you through their trials."

That didn't sound good.

"These trials would challenge you even if you were a hundred percent in control of yourself."

"And you don't feel I am now?" Because she needed him to believe in her. She was in way over her head and she was pretty sure she was the only one who knew that. Everyone else just needed her to deal with her shit and be done with it. Well, she...kinda needed that from everyone else in her family, too.

He narrowed his blue eyes, setting his teeth. "I fear that your child, if it is what I think it is, will unbalance you."

"And what's that?" She almost didn't want to know.

"I fear you carry a shifter-witch."

That wasn't all. She could smell it on him. "You also fear I am one."

"Yes. But Cawli balances you in a way your child will not be. There are many things we do not know about shifter-witches, but what we *do* know is that witches are capable of handling stronger shifter spirits. Your child has the potential to be extremely powerful."

All of the Whiskey kids were "extremely powerful." The idea of attacking those kids was a terrible one. Especially if they were together. Pity the fool who tried that.

"Were you to shift during your trials…"

A chill ripped through her body. Her first shift? In a foreign place? She really wanted Dexx and Chuck there with her if that happened. "Could we try it here?" she asked, her voice just above a whisper.

His lips flattened, but his eyes softened. "We don't have time," he said just as quietly. He scooted to the edge of his chair and held out his hands, palms up.

That could be a gesture, but she'd seen him make that same gesture to other members of his pack.

Of *his* pack.

She'd "been a part" of his pack since Texas, but as a witch. As an outsider.

She hadn't even realized she'd leaned forward and placed her fingertips in his.

The warmth of his hands as he curled his fingers around hers bolstered her courage.

She hadn't even realized just how terrified she was until that moment when the fear abated. So much hinged on her succeeding at all these things she sucked at. She wasn't a politician. She wasn't good at making friends or smoothing things over. She didn't have the silver tongue. She was a detective.

Chuck brought his head forward and clunked it lightly against hers in a very pack-gesture of support. "I have faith in you, Paige. You can do this, but you must be careful. The trials will push you to your limits."

Paige took in a shallow breath. "Will my baby be safe?" Saying the words out loud made her reality so much more real. Her baby. She was having another baby. Terror of losing this one like she'd lost her first one rippled through her like an emotional earthquake and her hands trembled.

Chuck squeezed her fingers. "It should be safe. But you cannot use your witch abilities on these shifters. You will want to."

Paige closed her eyes. "Do you want me to *lose?*" Because without her witch abilities, she would.

"Bring them back to our pack. I care less for what the Elder Council needs, but I want you in my region."

Paige raised her head.

Chuck met her gaze. "We need them, Paige. The safety of your family depends on it. If this child is what I think it is, we will need a very powerful pack to protect it."

Great.

Just great.

THREE

JUST WHAT PAIGE NEEDED. Another trip away from her responsibilities and her family.

She really needed to re-think this. If she was going to be spending this much time away from home, she had to find a replacement for something because she was being pulled in too many different directions. So, what was she going to give up?

Her role as an elder retriever? Yes. Absolutely.

Her role as Chuck's pack gatherer? Could she? That'd be lovely.

Her role as the leader of the Red Star Division? No. Just—no.

Her role as a mother?

That didn't even deserve an answer.

She *knew* she couldn't find someone else for the Elder Council or for Chuck, and she *refused* to give up on being a mom to her kids.

That only left finding her replacement at Red Star. Her being constantly away wasn't fair to Dexx or to her team.

But what about her kids? Was she going to find a replacement mom, too?

She sighed and unpacked her suitcase, putting in fresh clothes.

Leslie stepped into the doorway to Paige and Dexx's bedroom and leaned in, resting her shoulder on the hardwood and crossing her arms. "How long will you be this time?"

Paige shook her head. "I have no idea."

Leslie was quiet for a long moment.

Which gave Paige time to grab clean socks and underwear. Dexx had done the laundry. He was amazing in so many beautiful ways. She unmated her socks and mixed them up. He refused to mate them in unmatched pairs. Refused. But... he *had* washed and *folded* the laundry, so she wasn't going to complain. She dropped the now mismatched socks into the small suitcase.

"Remind me again what you're doin'?" Leslie's drawl deepened.

Meaning Leslie was getting pissed. "I don't know."

Leslie raised two very superior brown eyebrows over an expression of prim frustration.

Paige's flight wasn't for another three hours and the airport was literally right down the road from them. She shoved her laptop on top and zipped it closed. She had time and needed to talk. "You got a minute?"

"For my baby sister?" Leslie pushed off the doorway and turned, leading the way downstairs.

Paige slung the suitcase over her shoulder. It was one of those that could be a backpack, but could also roll. She'd perfected the art of packing light. She paused at the nursery, staring at the two empty cribs. They'd be getting toddler beds soon. She'd barely had a chance to *see* her son. He was always being taken care of by everyone else.

She stared up the stairs that led to the wide attic, picturing Leah and Mandy's room. She'd just won custody of Leah back and how much time had she actually spent with her daughter? Not a lot. It was one thing having a job that demanded a lot of hours. It was completely different when you had a job that you couldn't even define pulling you in so many directions it wasn't even funny. She needed to sit down with these guys and define some rules. She wanted some family time. Her *family* needed some family time. She was *supposedly* part of Dexx's pack, but it sure didn't feel like it. She felt owned. By the elders.

How had that happened?

She went downstairs and dropped her bag at the front door. Since Chuck was the one who really wanted this one-on-one with this Utah pack, so he'd offered to get her to the airport. That didn't mean he was going to drive her himself. Oh, no. But it did mean she could save money on parking.

She walked between the staircase leading up and the living room, heading to the large kitchen and dining room that took up half of the house.

Leslie was at the stove putting a kettle on the back burner. "Tea since coffee's bad for the baby."

Did *everyone* know? "How?"

Leslie gave her a lopsided grin and shrugged. "I'm guessing you haven't told Dexx."

Paige shook her head and took in a deep breath.

"Why not?"

Paige didn't have an answer. "I don't know. Scared?" But why would she be scared?

Because the man she loved was a free man who loved

the open road and hunting demons. She didn't want to be the thing that tied him down. She needed a distraction. "You're mad at me."

"I'm mad *for* you and disappointed that my baby sister isn't standing up for herself." Leslie opened the tea cupboard and pulled down a box. She showed it to Paige. "I got it for the baby."

Paige didn't even really look at it. She trusted Leslie with her life. And more.

"What's got you in such a spin over this, Pea?" Leslie filled a tea infuser and set it on the lip of a cup, then turned around. "I mean, I won't say this isn't like you. You've always been one to fall head-first into work. Work first, the rest of us second."

Which was true.

"But I really thought you'd turn that around once you got Leah back, and then with Bobby, and now this little one. Are you even going to take a break from work long enough to give birth?"

Paige didn't know. She leaned against the kitchen island —which had *finally* been screwed down—and gripped the granite counter top.

Leslie rolled her eyes and shook her head. "Tell me what's goin' on, at least."

That was the thing. There was a *lot* going on. "Demons in Portland."

"Know about that."

"What you don't know is how bad it is." Mostly because Paige hadn't wanted to alarm anyone. Everyone had their own mess to deal with and they all trusted that she'd clean up and manage hers. "Something big is going on. I don't know what. It's like the door to Hell is getting thinner."

"Great."

"Exactly. I don't know what it means."

"What about Balnore? He got any ideas?"

Balnore had been with Paige since she'd discovered she could summon demons. He was Giles to her Buffy, but he was a demon. Or something very close to that. She had never quite figured him out. However, he seemed to be able to keep his finger on the pulse of this uprising pretty well. "No, which was what we were trying to figure out in Portland last week."

"And the week before that?"

"Tracking down a demon who was going after drunk drivers who got away." Not all demons were bad, but they weren't gentle, either.

Leslie flicked her eyebrows and turned toward the kettle. It hadn't started whistling, but the water started hissing. She clicked off the burner and poured two cups. "And the weeks before?"

"Wasn't all demon stuff." Frankly, Paige had been pretty damned busy doing a lot of damned things.

"So, the elders have you working for them, too." That was almost a question, but not quite. Leslie handed Paige her cup and walked toward the large dining room table.

This table wasn't something you could buy at a store. It sat upwards of thirty people comfortably and sat diagonally in the wide, open room. One corner almost touched the green couch in the living room.

Paige sat next to her sister, facing the multi-paned window of the back door. No one was in the "back yard," or the meadow or the large...expanse of green. Whatever it was called. She could see the "arena" that Dexx had set up for the kids and his shifters.

She missed so much. What the hell was she doing?

Leslie's metal tea infuser clanked against her cup as she dunked it in and out of the water. She waited for Paige to talk on her own time.

She loved the hell out of Leslie. "I have a really bad feeling."

Leslie looked up at Paige, her expression calm.

This was something Paige hadn't told anyone. She didn't have the ability to tell the future. She could barely see past the end of her nose. "I just have a feeling that something horrible is just waiting on the edge of the horizon. I don't know what it is or what it means. I just know that something bad is waiting and I need to be ready."

"Okay." Leslie's tone was pleasant, her expression flat. "Does that justify leaving your kids? Your family?"

"I don't know." And Paige didn't, but she appreciated that Leslie was keeping her judgement to herself. "I shouldn't be bringing a baby into this. I know better."

Leslie took in a deep breath, her gaze shifting to the belly hiding beneath the table. "You could end it."

"I could. Well, I could have. I think I'm past that now."

Leslie hmm'd. "Did you think about it?"

"I had to. Didn't I? I mean, I'm sucking at being a mom now."

Leslie shrugged.

Paige bit her lips and stared into her mug. "Why did I fight so hard to get Leah here with us? I'm never here."

"If you're looking for a pity party, I'm not joinin' you." Leslie flattened her lips, her eyes wide as she shook her head, leaning back in her chair. "If you need to beat yourself up, sis, you do that way too well on your own and I'm not joining you."

So...Leslie thought she was doing the *right* thing?

"You do what you *need* to and you keep us safe."

Paige looked up at her sister. "That's what I'm trying to do."

"I know." Leslie shrugged. "You fought to bring your baby girl into the protective folds of your family and where is she the safest? Seriously."

"With all the danger I bring to her door? To the door of my son?"

"Have seen what our kids are capable of? They're not weak, Pea. And they're safer here under all of these wards, with Grandma and me and the pack and Chuck's pack and, I'm pretty sure if you asked it, the Blackmans would come to your aid, too. You can't forget they're your *family*."

Paige wanted to forget. Having the Blackman coven as her kin didn't give her the warm fuzzies.

Leslie slumped in her chair a little. "Whoever came up with the idea that women had to stay close to their kids in order to be a good mom was an asshole. When we need to, we have to protect our kids just as much as the men do."

That... was exactly what Paige needed to hear. "I still feel guilty."

"I feel guilty leaving my kids alone so I can cure a damned rabies virus for two days."

"I hear ya—wait. What?"

Leslie chuckled. "I kinda flew that one under the radar."

"What the hell are you *doing?* You're—" Paige struggled to find the right word. "Like a freakin' ninja."

"I don't think they'd appreciate you calling *me* a ninja."

"Okay. Super sneaky. Off saving the world. Wonder Woman."

"Hey." Leslie's face lit up in a tired smile. "I like that."

Paige sighed. "I've been so busy with demons and

saving the world, I haven't even asked you how you're doing. You seem busy."

"I am. The shifters are finally trusting me a little more. That helps. They're coming in when they're sick and don't want to go to Snow." She buried her neck up to her ears with her shoulders. "I'm happy and my kids are safe."

Something in her tone said otherwise.

Paige narrowed her eyes. "Do I want to know?"

Leslie shook her head. "Just Dexx."

"Oh." Paige groaned. "But they're all still alive."

"Yeah." Leslie said it almost hesitating.

"It's like letting kids eat dirt?" Paige gave her sister a pained expression. "To help them build their immune system."

"Oh, he's building their immunity to something." Leslie stood and stretched. "I've gotta head back to the shop. Barn's been holding down the fort for me, and if I'm going to make the rent this month, I need to make two new batches of soap. Special order and everything."

"Oh. Look at you." Paige stood. "Okay. Well, Chuck is swinging by to take me to the airport."

"Okay." Leslie wrapped Paige in a tight hug. "You take care of yourself. Okay?"

"Tell Leah I love her." Paige held Leslie close, relishing the warmth filling her soul.

"Always. Okay." Leslie pecked a loud kiss in Paige's ear. "I've gotta go because nap time is sounding a little too awesome. I'll give Bobby a wet sloppy kiss for you."

"Thank you."

Paige watched her sister leave and listened to the quiet of the Whiskey house.

This trip had damn well be worth it. Otherwise, she was

going to have a word with the Elder Council because she needed some damned downtime with her damned family.

With a growl, she picked up her backpack, her empty hand resting on her belly, and headed for the front door. She just had one more call to make.

Dexx.

FOUR

DEXX HADN'T BEEN HAPPY. He kept talking about how he was broken-hearted she hadn't brought him a sandwich, but she knew it was more than that. They really were better together.

The flight wasn't much to talk about. They took off on time, almost. Landed on time, almost.

The baby was getting to the point where things were starting to get uncomfortable. Oh, Paige had forgotten the joys that came with being pregnant. That was another thing that *might* help her eventually? At some point, she wouldn't be able to fly anymore. She *might* actually be able to take some time off and stay at home.

Wouldn't that be nice?

Not that she thought she'd get to spend much time at home. Probably not. She hoped to spend some time at Red Star.

But her reality was that she might have to find a replacement.

Would that be Dexx? Or someone else?

Probably someone else. She *loved* Dexx, but he wasn't

ready for this. In his heart, he was still a demon hunter who didn't have to obey the rules.

She followed the signs to Ground Transportation and stepped out onto the drive. She pulled out her phone to text the number Chuck had given her, letting her ride know that she was there and discovered she had three messages from Tuck and two from Chuck.

She couldn't even get off the plane?

She called Tuck back as she looked for column 12N. She had no idea what she was looking for because there were no further instructions. And... no further communication.

He answered on the second ring. "Flight okay?"

"Yeah. What's up?" She wasn't one for small talk and neither was he.

"Dexx is breaking my damned town," Tuck growled. "Do you have any idea how much a *mailbox* costs to replace it?"

"Wait. What happened?"

He then proceeded to inform her that Dexx had managed to get into a highspeed car chase in downtown Troutdale—something that...it really shouldn't happen. And that he'd somehow broken things up on the roof after the chase proceeded on foot.

"Oh." Paige had no idea what to do with him. She really didn't. "I'll call and will handle it."

"When are making it back?" He didn't sound any less grumpy.

"I don't know."

"Get a plan, Whiskey. I can't do this." The line went silent.

She understood he was talking about the need to find someone to run Red Star. She wasn't dumb.

She then called Chuck back who informed her that Dexx had an out-of-control shift on the rooftops. "We need Doe. Without them, Dexx will be in more danger of losing control of his shift."

No pressure.

She still didn't have a message from her driver nor did she see anyone pull up in front of her, so she called her baby-daddy. Yeah. She could call him that now.

How terrifying was *that* thought?

When she'd gotten a hold of Dexx finally, he tried to play it cool, but she wasn't buying it. "Tuck just called me. Did you have any problems today? Something you'd like to share?"

She could almost see the hamster inside his brain working double-time to get his brain to work. "No," he said finally. "Just had a slight disagreement with Hattie. I needed an extra push, and she gave me full cat. I need to put extra clothes in the car."

Except he was *supposed* to be handling that with Hattie. She talked to him a bit longer about it, but it was like talking to a small stack of bricks. A funny stack of witty bricks, but nothing she said changed one thought in his pretty head.

Midway through the conversation, her stomach flipped and she had to race to the bathroom to vomit. She didn't want to focus on the details, but this pregnancy was giving her some pretty weird morning sickness. Hers was afternoon sickness.

But instead of telling Dexx about her pregnancy, she blew it off as a bad taco. Again.

"Babe, you've been having a lot of bad tacos lately."

He wasn't wrong.

She told him she loved him and to be safe, knowing he'd

soak in the first part and ignore the last, then hung up to look for her ride, hoping she hadn't missed it.

Eventually, a silver SUV pulled in. It was one of the rounder-looking ones. Dexx would have the name for it. It wasn't a hybrid, but it was... sporty looking.

A man got out of the passenger seat and approached her. He was tall, wiry, and Middle-Eastern. His expression was neutral as he reached for her bag. "Paige Whiskey?"

"Guilty."

He flashed her a smile and turned, giving her a good view of his butt in those jeans. He wore boots and wore them in that bow-legged walk that some men had that was just damned sexy.

That was the *other* side effect of this pregnancy. Her sex drive was through the *roof. Did* she have anything to be worried about with this pregnancy? She was older now, almost forty. She hadn't gone in for a well-baby visit. No ultrasounds. No blood drawn.

Yeah. She should make an appointment when she got home.

If she managed to *stay* home long enough to make it.

The man opened the back door for her and headed toward the trunk to stash her bag. "I hope your flight was good."

He had zero accent which meant that for all his looks, he was plain-old American and probably from around here. "It was fine."

"Do you need anything before we get on the road? Food? Water? A restroom?" He closed the back hatch.

"Nope." She set her laptop bag on the far side of the seat and slid in, closing the door behind her.

He got into the front passenger seat. "Excellent. We're good," he said.

The driver had flaming red hair of the straight-out-of-a-bottle kind. But it was more than that. It was orange and green in spots. Galaxy hair. Paige was a little jealous. She would *love* to try that out. Though, she probably wouldn't go red. She wanted to go purple. The bright and vibrant color.

Paige forced a smile on her lips and buckled up. "Paige Whiskey."

"I figured," the driver said, getting into traffic.

"That's Kathy Bore," the man said. "I'm Mahir Uzun."

"Nice to meet you."

The vehicle filled with uncomfortable quiet as Kathy worked her way through traffic, getting them away from the airport. They took a highway that led off to some rather tall mountains.

So much flatness. Even the rolling prairies of Colorado weren't this damned flat.

Paige settled herself to watching out the window. She wasn't going to force conversation if they didn't want it. *She* was good with quiet.

The two up front didn't speak. They didn't turn on the radio, either.

Which was fine with Paige.

She had a million things she needed to work out. She hadn't really had the chance on the plane because she had a harder time thinking with so many people pressed against her as the pregnancy wore on. Smells were becoming more overwhelming. She could *taste* things on the air like emotions. She now understood how it was that all the shifters seemed to be able to read emotion. They tasted like crap.

She was worried about the demon uprising. Something was going on and damned if she could figure it out. Balnore had been "keeping his thumb on the pulse" for years, and she was getting a clearer and clearer picture that he hadn't done a great job of it.

Was this Sven? He'd kidnapped her almost a year and a half ago to carve a spell into her bones that opened a gate to Hell inside her soul. That had been a pretty hellish time. He and his cohorts had killed a lot of people. She didn't know which one was worse. Him, the demon, or his cohort Mike Jones, the angel? Which one had done more damage?

The more she thought about it, the more she had to think that maybe it was Mike Jones. She needed to put *him* back on her watchlist, too. Yeah. After Sven had slipped her nets, she'd gone looking for him. She'd found him—or rather, he'd found *her*—in Denver where Dexx, her partner and mate, had been bitten by a shapeshifter.

That's also where an animal spirit had invited himself in, weaving the door to Hell closed in her soul.

Yeah. That had kinda side-railed everything. Her hunt for Sven. Her need to chase down Mike Jones—even though, she wasn't an angel whisperer or summoner or really had much if any effect on them whatsoever.

But then when she'd discovered she'd inadvertently broken the treaty between shifters and witches by trying to save the shifters around Denver, things had detoured even more severely. She'd learned about the Eastwood witches, a massively strong coven who practiced blood magick.

And the coven leader had traipsed her happy ass to Texas.

Paige hadn't known if the woman was after Paige's family or not. It was possible. After all, Merry Eastwood had been the one who had *wanted* the war with the shapeshifters. She enjoyed imprisoning them and using them to *her* will. So, Paige had gone to Texas, reuniting with her family.

And won custody of her daughter back.

It was all very complicated, and Paige wasn't sure that any of those pieces actually tied back to the demon uprising. It might. It very well could be that the angels—or Sven—had used Paige's mother—the evil sadist—to take Leah and run, using the court of law to do it. Paige had...reacted poorly and had raised a demon to murder the woman.

And Balnore had elicited Alma's help to banish Paige's memories and gifts.

For years.

Yeah. Paige guessed that *maybe* Leah could be a part of the demon uprising because while Paige had been out of commission, the demon population had grown unchecked.

But now Paige was back. Well, kind of. She'd inherited a baby boy, thanks to some angels who probably had no frelling idea what they were doing, and had moved her entire family to Oregon, back to the old homestead.

And then she'd taken Merry Eastwood down.

With the covens no longer providing a problem and the threat of war no longer at her door, Paige was able to concentrate on demons.

Well, and helping the Elder Council reclaim some of the territories it had lost thanks to the wars.

She was starting to be more of a damned politician than anything else and that unnerved her. Paige didn't know the first damned thing about *being* a politician. It was all about reading people and then playing the room.

She was a little too tactless for that.

Or so she'd thought.

Turned out, she was a bit better at it than she'd hoped she would be.

Maybe better than she was a detective.

And that hurt because she'd worked her ass off at that job for almost twenty years. Okay. Closer to fifteen, but at that point, weren't you allowed to just round?

"We're almost there." Kathy's voice was mellow, her words succinct but not sharp.

"Okay. Thanks."

"I gotta question, if it doesn't piss you off."

"Kathy," Mahir warned quietly.

"It's okay." Because Paige was there to help improve relations. Goddess bless, she *hoped* she didn't frell it up. But she'd been doing pretty good. She'd even met elves. Frelling elves and she'd done okay, so she *should* do just fine with this as well.

Cawli purred contently in the back of Paige's mind, offering a quiet support without being fully engaged in the moment.

"What kind of witch are you?" Kathy asked.

Paige had been asked that question a lot. At first, it had thrown her because she didn't know what they were asking. And, really, they didn't know either. What they wanted to know was if she was good or bad or had the potential to be bad. "Well, I'm a decent human being who doesn't go out and fuck people over on a whim."

Kathy looked at the rearview mirror, but they couldn't see each other.

"And besides that, I'm a witch. I have life, death, and door magick."

Mahir sighed and resituated in his seat.

Paige wished she could see his face, but she could tell that her answer didn't please him.

"But it's a little like having a really big man with bulging muscles having the talent to punch people in the face and then break it." She'd met more than a few men like that. Women, too. "It depends on the person, not the abilities."

Kathy nodded and slowed. "Well, I'm a wolf."

"I think my animal is a cat."

She narrowed her eyes. "So, it's true."

"It is."

"Do you shift?"

"Nope."

"Then, how do you know it's a cat?"

That was an excellent question. "Because he purrs and when he speaks, he has a male voice."

"Oh."

Mahir took in a sharp breath. "He speaks to you."

"Yes." When an animal spirit talked to their human host, some said that meant they were an alpha. However, Paige was fairly certain there was something more to it than that. "He's...well, he keeps me on the straight and narrow."

"You can understand why we would be concerned, don't you?" Kathy turned on a gravel road that seemed to lead into the desert.

During the wars Merry Eastwood had started over two hundred years before—yes, two hundred years—witches and shifters had done some pretty horrible things to one another.

But only in this region. Everywhere else, witches and shifters worked together just fine.

"I've heard that were I able to shift, I would be able to choose any shape I wanted." Which didn't sound like a horrible thing. It actually sounded pretty damned cool and not something to be scared of.

"Yeah. And they're more powerful."

But that was all rumor. "No one's seen a shifter witch in generations."

Mahir snorted.

Oh, great. She was showing her ignorance again. "Okay. Well, I can't shift and Cawli is just here for support. He helps me and I help other shifters when and where I can."

Kathy made a noise.

The road dropped into a deep gulch that was hard to see from the road. A wide river meandered along the bottom and green blossomed in the wide beaches and farmlands protected by the towering walls.

"It's beautiful." Paige couldn't help herself.

"Well, it's ours."

Oh, goodness. Two-year-old emotions. Great. "You'll have to come to our place sometime so you can see. It's gorgeous there, too. It's just different. This is like a protected gem in a sea of sand."

Kathy raised her eyebrows and glanced at Paige over her shoulder before concentrating on the narrow, winding road. "You can keep your poetry. I'm not buyin' what you're sellin'."

"That's good." Paige watched the scenery outside her window, staring down the chasm as far as she could through the trees that grew closer and closer together. "Because I'm not sellin'."

"We'll see about that."

Oh, yeah. This was going to be amazing.

FIVE

KATHY PULLED up in front of an tiny house. It wasn't small exactly, but when compared to all the other houses Paige seen shifters live in, it was rather dinky. It looked, for all intents and purposes, like a normal track house. It had two floors, with two windows on the front, and two gables up top. She had no idea how an entire pack of shape shifters could possibly live here.

They didn't all need to live there. They could be like the Whiskeys and have separate houses in the back. Of course, she didn't really know how Chuck's pack worked. Did anyone know how Chuck's pack worked?

Kathy and Mahir got out of the car and headed up to the front door.

Paige decided to leave her bags there for now because who knew what she was going to be facing? She pulled herself out of the car and followed.

Before they'd even made it up the stairs, a woman stepped out. She was probably a good inch taller than Paige and had long black hair. Her features were sharp, and her eyes were dark. Paige couldn't tell what color they were.

Paige stopped at the bottom of the stairs, looking up. "Hey. I'm Paige Whiskey."

"Figured as much." The woman's voice was soothing. It didn't grate on the nerves, wasn't high-pitched, and didn't have any kind of tinny sound that sometimes came with old age or smoking. Not that Paige thought she was going to hear a tinny voice, but she sometimes just never knew. In her travels, she had discovered that shifters and the paranormal's at large lived a very hard life. That hard life sometimes affected their voice.

"Okay." Paige shoved her hands in her pockets. Well, as far as her female cut pockets allowed. Meaning, she was able to shove her fingertips to the first knuckle. "Are we going to stand here and talk all day? Are we going to dance, maybe?"

The woman smiled. "You've got some spunk."

Oh, if she only knew. "With the things I've seen and the people I've met, spunk is the best thing I've got right now."

The woman narrowed her gaze. "Yeah?"

Paige shook her head not quite knowing what she was supposed to say. She probably shouldn't be spilling her guts about a whole bunch of stuff, but at the same time she needed to tell these people that everything was going to be okay. And the only way to do that was to let them know that she was normal. Well, normal kind of. She was still a very powerful witch and she was housing the spirit animal inside her. But she still put her pants on like everyone else, and she was still capable of being tired as fuck after getting off of an airplane. Again. "Let's start with your name."

The woman straightened a smile forming on her lips. "Dorothy Raines."

Paige raised her eyebrows in surprise. Dorothy was one of those names that had kind of died out. But she'd always liked it. What the heck were they going to name *their* child? If she came out a girl, was Dorothy even on the list? Dexx would probably strike it. But that was something they were going to have to discuss. "So, you go by Dorothy or do people call you something else?" Because she was pretty sure there were very few people who actually went by Dorothy.

The other woman smiled again. "They call me Doe. Well, at least we can say you're observant."

"That's probably the nicest thing anybody said to me in a good long while. Well, at least during introductions."

Doe folded her hands in front of her. "I take it you haven't been receiving a warm reception."

Paige laughed. "Warm reception? No."

Doe studied her for a while and then gestured away from the house. "Take a walk with me."

That certainly wasn't the worst idea ever. Paige stepped aside to let Doe pass and then kept pace with her.

The woman led her into an orchard. The trees lined up in long rows. The leaves were out and they were flowering. However, Paige had no idea what type of trees they even were. It was time to break the ice. "What kind of trees are these?"

Doe looked around, and then shrugged. "These are peach. Cherry are down the way. This is a great location for orchards."

Not that this was horrible information, it just wasn't what Paige was there for. She hadn't left her kids at home so she could talk about fruit. She *did* have to watch how focused she could be during conversations because people *did* talk about unimportant things when they needed a space to be *human*. This was her weak point when it came to politics. In political situations, the conversations had to be fluid. She kept her sigh of frustration to herself and said instead, "Peach is my favorite fruit."

"Have you ever had a peach fresh off the tree?"

Paige shook her head. "I guess I'm a bit too much of a city girl. Now, I've gone to the farmers markets. I've purchased peaches that were perfectly ripe. *Those* were amazing."

Doe clasped her hands behind her back, continuing to walk. "Maybe one day you'll have an opportunity to eat one fresh off the tree."

Paige didn't quite know if that was an invitation, or if she was just trying to tell Paige to put that on her bucket list. "I hope to do that."

Doe slowed her pace. "You understand that we have reservations about you."

Paige tipped her head to the side, smelling the sweet scent of the blossoms and something else, something... earthy. "I *had* received that memo."

"The thought that you could be a shifter witch is terrifying. To think that you could have all that power—it makes the rest of us feel as though we have a new enemy on our front."

Oh, they had a new enemy. It just wasn't Paige. "I guess I don't understand. If I'm on your side, how can you continue to be afraid of me?"

Doe didn't answer immediately. "There are stories passed down about witches who were bitten and became shifter witches. The ones who started out as witches were brutal enough, but they were outside the pack and the packs had *some* protections. But the ones who were *inside* a pack?" Doe shivered. "They *destroyed* their packs from the inside."

Wait. "There are other witches inside of packs?"

"Not..." Doe lifted a shoulder and let it drop. "...here, but the rules are different in other parts of the world. New Zealand, the UK, Australia. Those are just the ones I know of. But there are others. Elsewhere. You're not unique, Ms. Whiskey. You're just dangerous."

She really wasn't. "I'm not here to do you any harm."

"I need to see that for myself."

"And you're really going to pull your pack from the region?"

Doe stopped and studied Paige. "Do you have any idea what it means to be a part of the regional protection?"

Paige really didn't. Dexx might. After all, he was spending a lot more time with the shifters. Paige, however, has been spending her time everywhere else. "No. I don't."

Doe lowered her gaze. "How much time have you actually spent with shape shifters?"

Paige really wished that she could say she'd spent a lot, but she couldn't. So, it was time to be honest. "I've spent most of my time with demons."

Doe's gaze jerked up.

Yeah. It was time to let her know exactly what it was that Paige was dealing with. "I'm a demon summoner." Paige turned and walked off at a slow pace.

Doe moved to keep up.

"You have no idea what's even brewing on the horizon." Frankly, neither did Paige. "Demon populations have been on the rise, and there's very little I've been able to do about it. I'm less concerned with shape shifters and witch shifters —or whatever and more concerned with the demons. And the *angels* that come with them. There's a war coming and it will be fought in *our* backyards. And I have no idea what to do to stop it. That's what *I* care about."

Doe shook her head.

At least she was listening. "You and Chuck care about your packs. I get that. I do. But I've got a kid who's being hunted—*hunted*—by demons *and* angels because he can tell *their* future. I've got one kid who can raise the dead because she's got powerful door *and* blood *and* life magick flowing in her veins. And you want to tell me that *you're* scared because I could be carrying a child who could choose her shape? At will?" Paige snorted. "Look... Doe. I'm sorry, but there's a bigger, badder war just waiting to be set off and me being *here* isn't helping."

"Then why *are* you here?"

Oh, fuck. Paige licked her lips. "Because Chuck asked me. Because by letting me and Dexx and the rest of the Whiskeys into his pack, he's off centered? Unbalanced in his alpha power?"

"He's giving his power to you to keep *you* stable."

Paige hoped Doe understood that better than she did. "I guess. But if he kicks us out..." Paige didn't *want* to think about that. She *wanted* to ignore it.

She couldn't. If they were kicked out, her kids would be displaced. Again. Her family could lose their jobs. Again. They'd still have the house. Well, for as long as they could afford the payments on the loan they'd taken to build their house. But... what would they do if the town turned their backs on the Whiskey clan?

Because of her?

Something in Doe's expression said she *did* understand a little too well.

What *exactly* was going on here?

Doe ducked her head, and then looked up again. "That sounds fine and all, and scary, but how can I believe you?"

"How about you use my current track record?" Paige stopped, trying to figure out what she wasn't seeing. Maybe there was *more* to her being there than just her unborn child. But what was it? Maybe Doe had a witch friend who'd been bitten? Maybe she needed to know if her friend could be saved? That gave Paige a tiny thread of hope. "Every single time I turn around, I'm being pulled away for something. Whether it's to hold a shifter pack's hand, or another paranormal community's hand, or to go fight demons and keep an eye on angels."

Doe folded her arms over her chest.

"Do you have any idea how much time I've actually been able to spend with my family?" That was probably a bad line to take. Redirect. "I'm not whining. Don't think that I am. But I need you to understand, that if I could spend less time reassuring people that I'm a pretty okey-dokey person, then I could concentrate fully on the issue at hand. *This* is not the issue at hand. The demons are."

Doe raised an eyebrow. "That's one helluva speech."

"It's not a speech."

"Okay. Then why *are* you here? Because Chuck asked you to come? If you *really* think this is a waste of your time..." Doe let that conversation thread drop with a shrug.

It was a damned good question. "He asked in this..." How could she put it into words that wouldn't scare Doe away? "I'm powerful. I know that. I'm leading people and I'm doing... well, I'm failing less each day. But Chuck..." Paige sucked with words as her heart pushed forward with a complex twist of emotions. "I look up to him and it's *nice* having someone I *can* look up to, who *is* my leader." She ran the tip of her tongue along the roof of her mouth and released a long breath. "Sounds dumb. I know."

"It doesn't." Doe turned away, rubbing the back of her neck. "You don't know what it means to be part of his pack?"

Paige let her gaze drop. Because this was something she needed to work on. "I wasn't bitten. My spirit animal chose me with a bite. He and I are not connected the same way you are. Not like we're supposed to be. He's bridging the door to Hell that's embedded in my soul. Keeping it sealed."

Doe took a step back.

Paige wondered if Doe even realized she'd done that. "Yeah it's bad. And yet one more reason why I need to be back chasing demons and not sitting here making sure that your tender feelings are okay."

"They're not tender feelings." Doe took a step forward straightening. Her resolve settled like steel to her spine.

There *was* something else going on here and Paige just had to figure out what that was. "Good, because if it was, this would be a complete waste of time. Look, I'm here to make sure that you feel comfortable with me—" If she was *right* then this had less to do with *her* and more to do with what she was, but for *other* reasons. "...with shifter witches being around. We need you to be a part of the community. Chuck's only concern isn't himself. He wants to make sure you're as protected as possible, too. That's it. The end. But whatever this is—" She gestured to the both of them. "—needs to settle quickly because I'm not where I need to be."

Doe looked back towards the house and raised her chin. She was silent for a long moment and then turned her attention back to Paige. Her expression was firm and unforgiving. "I understand that you feel that you're in the wrong place right now, but you're exactly where *I* need you to be. So, you either settle in and get comfortable or you can go."

"Oh, I'm staying. But don't waste my time because we don't have any extra to be wasting." Paige was starting to get a little bit pissed. Well, maybe not quite pissed, but her feathers were getting ruffled.

"I'm going to be putting you through several trials."

Paige was waiting for new information.

"I have five alphas."

Paige sighed. Great. She had a feeling she knew where this was headed.

"You will need the votes from at least four of them."

Awesome.

"It won't just be about performance, Ms. Whiskey. You'll be learning things you need to know in order to be a part of a shifter community."

"I've been in one for almost a year."

"You've been *near* a community, and the member of a pack, but on the outside." Doe raised an eyebrow. "We need to see how you perform within one, which is where you need to be."

Where Paige needed to be? Or someone else?

Doe let her arms fall to her sides. "I will let you get yourself settled, and then you're going to the Spirit Cave to see if you're even going to participate in any trials. You may not make it."

A Spirit Cave. Well, that sounded rather ominous

"Since you're in such a hurry, let's get started."

Yeah. She should do that thing. Because Paige seriously had no idea what was waiting for her at home.

SIX

THE DIRECTIONS to the Spirit Cave were a little less than amazing. It didn't even include a map. And of course, Cawli was quiet on the entire trip. Paige was basically out wandering in the desert by herself without a clue on where to go.

Paige didn't really do well just sitting around in her own brain space. Unfortunately, she had entirely too much of that lately. On plane trips, car trips, empty hotel rooms, her computer, and a TV. She had entirely too much time to think. She really didn't need any more of that.

Kathy drove her out to the middle of nowhere, and then dropped her off by an outcropping of rocks. The stone face looked jagged and somehow fresh. But that didn't make any sense.

Dexx might know what they were. He claimed to know a lot about rock and geology, or geography, or whatever people who studied rocks were.

Paige had spent the last hour going over each and every single one of those rocks trying to find a cave, but had found absolutely nothing. The sun had gone down, the stars were out, and it was starting to get a little chilly.

She sat down on one of the rocks and lay back, looking up at the Milky Way. When was the last time she'd actually looked at the Milky Way? She couldn't remember. All of the stars. It reminded her of just how small her little life was in the great universe. Well, they weren't that small. Her problems were demons. They weren't the spelling bee.

What was she doing out here? She had no idea what was going on at home. Granted, she hadn't received another phone call from Chief Tuck, but that didn't necessarily mean anything. It could just be that Dexx was hiding his level of crap.

What had he got mixed up in?

Where was Quinn?

Who had framed Rainbow?

Who had framed *Dexx*?

Why did it feel familiar in a messed up way?

What the hell was going on with her team?

And why the hell was she out in the middle of the desert staring up at the stars doing absolutely nothing when her entire team needed her at home?

The stars weren't giving her any answers.

She knew that if she went back now, first of all, it would be a really long walk. Second, of all she'd be lost, and thirdly she'd lose. But did she care? Really, did she *really* care? She'd been sent out there for someone else's business.

Except that Chuck said he needed the shifter group to help keep *her* family safe.

How many times was she going to fall for that line of BS?

Every time, probably.

Sighing, she sat up and then wished she hadn't. Baby.

Okay, so granted the baby wasn't that big, but it was already starting to shift parts around. They were in the beginning stages being uncomfortable. Her pants were getting tight, and her bladder was letting her know that maybe she shouldn't bend down to tie her shoes. Which was the reason why she was wearing slip-ons all the time.

"Oh, baby," she said, rubbing her belly, "I have no idea how I keep getting us into situations like this. What kind of world am I bringing you into?"

As she sat there staring off into the growing darkness seeing nothing but dark shadows of hills and cactuses and the bright lights of the stars high in the sky, something flashed in her peripheral vision. She turned to the right to see if she could get a glimpse of it, but whatever it was already disappeared. Honestly, it could be coyotes.

Something moved to her right again.

She stood up, turning. Whatever it was, it was moving.

She didn't hear any yips, didn't hear any gravel or sand moving with footsteps. So, what was out there?

Spirits of departed people?

She almost chuckled to herself but then stopped because she was one of the few people that actually knew that ghosts were real.

She didn't have a gun. She didn't have a knife. The only thing she had with her were her senses, her powers, and a really quiet spirit animal that was absolutely no help whatsoever in *any* kind of situation.

Cawli stirred in the back of her head. *I heard that.*

"Good. Because I'm standing out in the middle of the desert because of you."

I doubt it is because of me.

"You're right. Technically, it's not, however, I'm a shifter because of you."

Normally, when she let slip something like that, he would immediately tell her that she could not shift. He had never explained to her why it was that she couldn't, but he'd always made it quite clear that she would never be able to shift her shape.

"Cawli," Paige said quietly, "what haven't you been telling me?"

Things are a lot more complicated than you might imagine.

"No, I think I get just how complicated things are. You know how I know that? Because I've got a huge mess that I'm attempting to clean up."

You have not been trying to clean this one up.

"Well, if you let me know what the issue is, perhaps I can help."

Something shifted just ahead of her, a shadow among shadows scurrying from one rock to the next. She couldn't even tell what kind of shape it was.

The figure moved silently. From one rock to another, without shifting pebble or crunching gravel.

She'd seen a ghost before, but it wasn't a shadow. Demons could look like a shadow, but couldn't hide what they were. Whatever this new thing was, it wasn't one of those.

She pulled her witch hands out, preparing for an attack. She gathered power for lightning. At least then she could see.

Cawli growled slightly as if under his breath, if that was even possible. *Let me,* he said.

He crept forward in her consciousness and suddenly the shadows disappeared. Well, they didn't necessarily disappear, they just looked different. There were colors, and she could see depth. She could see the formation of the rocks and how deep they were. She could see the bushes in the cactuses, and she could make out a mouse on the ground not too far from her."

"You've been hiding this for me."

You've never needed it before.

"And here I thought we were partners."

He said nothing.

"Okay so what's out there?" Paige took her new sense of sight and scanned the area, trying to find the mysterious figure she kept seeing but only fleetingly. "Is it a coyote?"

It is not a coyote.

"Are you really going to make me guess?" She kept her eyes peeled on the area where she had last seen the figure. She just needed it to pop out one more time so she could see. Was it human? Was it an animal? Was it a ghost?

It almost felt as if Cawli had gotten up in the back of her mind and was pacing. She would never get used to that. *It is your spirit guide.*

"My spirit guide? So, this is the real thing? And we're actually going to find this cave?"

Cawli huffed like only a big cat can. *You can only find the spirit cave entrance with the spirit guide's help.*

"Great." Not great. "So, what are we waiting for? Let's get the show on the road. People to save, worlds to change, and spirits to impress."

She moved up the hill towards the outcropping of rocks where she had seen the shadow thing. As she drew closer, the shadow moved off to her right. She moved in that direction and followed the shadow from rock to rock up to the massive hill. She'd been in that location just two hours before. However, instead of a huge rockface like she'd seen and felt before, she now saw the gaping maw of the cave.

To her cat's eyes, the opening gave off a blue light, and

pulsed slightly. Following, she decided to try Cawli one more time. *Is this a good idea?*

He didn't answer her immediately. *It's the only idea.*

What do you mean by that?

You will see.

It was obvious she wasn't going to get any more answers from Cawli, so Paige stepped into the massive cavern.

Once inside, she looked around, staring at the walls in amazement. The walls glowed, blue and black, like the night sky but the stars were all wrong in their positions. She could make out the Milky Way, and distorted constellations but much brighter. They lit up the cave well enough for her to see without Cawli's vision.

Towards the back was a very large, clear lake. Well, the water around the edges was clear, but as the water grew deeper, it became a brilliant color of glowing blue.

She didn't know what else to do, so she walked towards the lake. The little shadow figure had gone, and she still never figured out what shape it had taken. There was a flat rock along the edge. So, she did the only thing that made any sense. She sat down. No one spoke to her. No one came. It was just her and the glowing walls and lake.

She had been walking and her shoes weren't designed for that many miles.

She was ready to take them off, and she had a brilliant lake of what looked to be clear, cool water right in front of her. She pulled off her boots, pulled off her socks, and dipped her toes, waiting for Cawli to tell her that she shouldn't be doing that.

However, the only thing he did was pace in the back of her mind.

What was going on?

The moment her toes touched the water the cool water,

peace overwhelmed her. She leaned on her hands and let her head fall backwards as she stared into the sky on the rock ceiling. She opened herself to the room around her, knowing that it was just her and Cawli and Cawli already knew the worst things about her. She didn't have to worry about him. He accepted her. Even knowing all of her faults.

The air warmed.

Paige pulled herself up and looked out in front. Rising from the luminescent water rose a magnificent mammoth. He rose so high above the water that it looked as if his massive head would touch the ceiling that was several feet above her. His head swung from side to side as he moved forward, but the water didn't ripple with his footsteps. He made no sound as he approached.

Paige didn't know what to do. She just sat there, waiting. But something inside her said to stay calm and everything would be okay.

And then she realized that that feeling was from Cawli. And he was again oddly quiet.

The mammoth stopped directly in front of her and reached out with his trunk as if to feel her face.

Paige let him, and then reached up to touch what was so amazingly real. She could even feel the saliva or snot from his nostrils. And she really didn't want to think about the slime, because it was gross. Elephant neat. Snot gross. Her fingers felt the coarseness of his hair. It really was hair. There was no way that this was fur. She could feel his skin. And he was warm.

Paige Whiskey. The mammoth's voice was big, booming, and comforting.

She just looked into one of his eyes. One of his massive, electric blue eyes. "Yes?"

Do you know why you are here?

It was time to be honest, because this might be the only chance she had to get real answers. "The local pack told me that I needed to be here. And then I'm supposed to enter into some kind of trials tomorrow. Chuck says he needs them in his region. He feels something big coming, and he feels that he needs them."

All of that, but do you know why you *are here?*

That was a good question. "I need answers."

The mammoth pulled his head up and raised his trunk releasing an elephant trumpet she had never heard before. It was big and deep and rattled the rafters. The rock underneath her butt jiggled a dance to the power of his voice.

She probably should be afraid. However, she just wasn't. She didn't know if it was Cawli or if it was something else, but she just couldn't fear this massive, amazing creature.

Paige stood, digging her toes into the soft sand of the Spirit Lake. "Cawli has been keeping secrets from me. I don't necessarily need to know *what* he's hiding, I just need to know why."

And why do you need to know this?

Paige bowed her head. What reason could she give such a powerful spirit animal? In this room of stars. She turned around, staring up into them, feeling small but knowing that her problems were much bigger. "I'm in over my head," she said, her throat constricting with the threat of tears.

She didn't even know where those were coming from. Under normal circumstances, she would curse and she would push those tears away, and she would force herself to be strong. But right then, staring up at the stars and talking with an extinct animal of this gargantuan size, she just couldn't. She knew her life relied on her honesty.

And that honesty came with tears. Tears that maybe she hadn't been willing to even share with herself.

"I have so many different things coming at me." She had no idea what she was supposed to say. "My kids are being threatened from every angle, and I have no way of knowing how to keep them safe. I thought that pulling my family together would keep them safe, but it only seems to have focused everybody's attention on us. Every single week it seems like we're being attacked by something else."

The mammoth flicked his trunk.

"We have demons and angels. What am I supposed to do with those? And this door to Hell inside my soul?" She turned to the mammoth who had lowered his trunk back into the water and remained still, watching her. "I am grateful that Cawli helped me close that. I wouldn't even want to see what the world would be like if he hadn't."

Then what are your questions?

This might be her only chance to get the questions she had answered. The only thing was, she hadn't even allowed herself to ask the questions to herself.

"Why does Cawli say I can't shift?"

She really hadn't intended to ask that particular question because she didn't need to shift.

The mammoth tipped his head to the side, studying her. *He offered you a chance he should not have.*

"Is it because of witch shifters?"

Yes. They are too powerful, and they can do great damage to not just the spirit animals but also to our spirit plane.

Well, that was certainly news. "I have no intention of doing that."

But what of your babies? Those which grow inside your belly?

Babies? As in plural? Holy crap. "It's not as if they're being born evil."

Are you sure?

"Pretty sure." They were babies.

The mammoth huffed a huge sigh and looked away slamming his trunk against the water and splashing her. *Unfortunately, the situation has been taken out of our control. Your family has already been blessed with more shifter spirits than we are comfortable with.*

Paige sincerely didn't want to hurt anybody. Well, except for the demons. She wanted to kick their little asses. And the angels. If she could find some way to kick them off this planet and never see them again, she would do it in half heartbeat. Well, most of them. "The Whiskeys will not hurt you or your kind."

I certainly hope not. The mammoth stepped back, sinking into the lake. *For our sakes.*

Well, at least he didn't say as *well as yours.*

A lot of trust is being given to you, Paige Whiskey. Make sure you're worthy of it. And then the massive mammoth disappeared into the lake. The lake evaporated, the cave dissolved, and she was standing by the road where she was meant to get her ride back to her house.

Without her shoes.

Awesome.

SEVEN

THE SUN WAS STARTING to light up the sky as Paige stood by the side of the dirt road waiting for her ride. The stars slowly winked out, the darkness creeping to a sheen of pink and lighter blue.

Cawli, I didn't get the answers I wanted.

The big cat sighed, but crept forward. *I know.*

What aren't you telling me? Because she was starting to get a feeling this was so much bigger than anything she could have ever guessed.

He seemed to curl up in her mind, settling close. *Not all of us believe we need to keep the witches at a safe distance.*

I don't know what that means.

*It means...*He trailed off and then began again after a pregnant pause. *There are certain spirits that have been forced to stay in the spirit plane.*

Why?

Because they are too powerful.

What the hell did that even mean? *Like... Dexx and Hattie?*

No. What they have is entirely different. They've been connected for lifetimes.

Okay. Dexx? Seriously. *Then, what are you talking about?*

Like the mammoth.

Why the hell was he being so damned cryptic? *So, you're telling me...what? My kid could potentially bond with the wooly mammoth?* That would make shifting in town awkward.

There are others. Cawli settled his massive head on his paws. *Spirits that cannot be bonded to weaker people.*

Like what?

Like the gryphon and the thunder bird and other creatures who have disappeared from existence.

They were spirit animals?

Bonded to witches and sorcerers, yes.

Wow. This was...neat.

There are many of us who think the time of the ancients has arrived again.

The time of the—that could be awesome. Except... *What do you see coming?*

Something big.

Still cryptic.

We cannot see into the future, little one.

That was the first time he'd called her by a pet name.

I had been following you and your sister for years before you came to visit Sam.

After she'd had the door to Hell branded into her soul, she'd discovered the world of shifters and vampires and other paranormals. She'd met a shaman named Sam and shortly after that, Cawli had introduced himself to her in the form of a cloud. He'd bonded to her without a bite, and then she'd been able to resume her ability to deal with demons.

She'd always been grateful.

But a part of her it always wondered what the real reason had been. She realized that a part of her was a bit cynical. Callous maybe, but she just didn't believe that people did things out of the kindness of their own hearts anymore. And that included animals.

"What's really going on here? Why did you really choose me?"

Cawli was silent.

"You didn't choose me because I was a good fit."

Cawli turned his head on his paw.

"You didn't choose me because I had a good heart."

I did choose you because you had a good heart.

"How's that even possible? I admitted to you what I had done." And she had. She'd just gotten off the phone with Rachel, her mother, and she'd been pissed. In that moment, she'd been so angry, she'd wanted to hurt Rachel.

If she'd met Cawli after she'd seen the photos of Leah Rachel had finally sent, he'd have seen her even more angry. Rachel had promised to send photos of Leah, and she had. But with Rachel's name branded over Leah's face or very near it in every photo.

She hadn't been drawn to summon a demon to kill Rachel that time. Paige'd been tempted to buy a plane ticket so she could punch the woman in the face personally.

But Cawli had chosen her anyway.

There are many things you do not understand about the animal kingdom.

"We have time." She could see far into the distant horizon and there was nothing. For miles. "Why don't you teach me?" She wasn't requesting.

Cawli stood and faced her inside of her own mind. *You humans have so many rules that mean absolutely nothing.*

Paige didn't quite think she believed that, but she decided she was going to keep her mouth shut for the moment.

Sometimes, in order to do what is right, one must do what feels wrong. Or, one must do something that others would tell you is wrong in order to do what is right.

Paige didn't like where this is going.

So, when you admitted what you had done, I did not judge you as a human would. I saw you as an animal would, and the only thing I found lacking was that Rachel remained breathing.

Well, that was oddly refreshing. And reassuring. "Thank you. I think."

Refreshing or not, that is why I chose you.

There's just something in the way he said that, in his tone maybe? "I think you're lying."

No. His tone was full, rich. *I am not.*

"Okay, then it wasn't the only reason."

No. It was not.

Okay? Was he going to make her guess?

I introduced you to the spirit animal world in the hopes that other spirit animals would allow your family in on their own.

"And did they?"

Your sister was bitten, wasn't she?

"By a kid. Not a real alpha."

It doesn't really matter. This is one of the reasons why we keep our children safe within the confines of the paranormal community.

"And here I thought it was to keep the society safe."

It is. But not in all of the ways that you think.

"So my sister is a shape shifter."

Yes.

That piece of information was like a punch to the gut.

And then something clicked. Leslie had been bitten months before. If she hadn't manifested any signs until now, what did that mean? "So, when Chuck was talking about the power that was growing inside of his pack, he wasn't talking about my baby." Babies.

Oh, he was talking about them as well.

"But Leslie, too."

Yes.

"Why are you being so secretive about this?"

Because the council of ancients has told me I cannot tell you anything.

"But you and I are partners."

Which is why I'm bending the rules a little. Since I've chosen you, a few other ancients have ventured into the world of their own free will. There are other shifter witches in the world who are chosen.

The way he emphasized that last word made it feel like there were other ways to become a shifter witch.

Something incredibly powerful has chosen your sister.

Paige'd been around long enough to realize that sometimes when people said "powerful," what they really meant was deadly scary. And when one person grew in power, opposing forces typically rose to counter it.

This creature hasn't been seen in millennia.

"Tell me she's a unicorn." She was joking. She hoped that unicorns were cute and fuzzy and everything that every unicorn-loving child ever dreamed of. But she had a feeling, like a terrible rumbling in her lower intestine, which actually could be gas, that unicorns were more powerful than anybody had anticipated or thought. After all, they had disappeared with all the other big mythological creatures like trolls and dragons.

It's not a unicorn.

Paige didn't know if she should be excited about that or not.

The being who chose her is much more powerful than the unicorn.

Oh, crap. "What do I need to be worried about?"

A dust cloud rose off to Paige's left. Kathy was finally on her way.

Let's just say that Chuck was right.

"In what way?"

We need this pack. Leslie and the ancient who chose her are going to need all the help you, your pack, and Chuck's regional pack can offer.

"Or what?"

Cawli turned his face toward the approaching car. *Let's just say there was a reason the ancients were forced off the face of this earth.*

Kathy drew closer in a cloud of dust.

Paige was still upset she'd lost her boots.

"So, what do I do?"

Cawli turned and padded towards the back of Paige's mind. *You do everything in your power to bring that pack in. We will need her and as many others as we can find. What's coming to your aid* – The way he said that word made it sound like it wasn't really aid. – *will need all the help he can get. But...also teach her what she needs to know.*

Paige'd been right. *She has a shifter witch.*

Cawli was gone.

Kathy pulled the car up beside Paige and dust settled around them.

Paige opened the door and sank into the passenger seat silently.

Kathy didn't immediately put the car in gear. She glanced down at Paige's feet. "What happened to your boots?"

Paige breathed in a large breath. "They were left behind."

Kathy bit down on her bottom lip and then put the car in gear using the shifter between them. "I can't tell you how many people have done that."

Paige realized that what she really needed to do was to talk to Kathy, to see what she could do about bringing the shifter pack in by strengthening communication.

But Cawli had just dropped a bombshell on her. She wasn't much in the talking mood.

"The water is amazing, isn't it?"

Paige let her head fall back as she stared out her window, watching the desert pass by. "It was."

"Which spirit animal did you see?"

Paige turned to look at Kathy. "There's a different one each time?"

"Of course. We see who we need to."

Spirit caves. "Okay. Who did you see?"

Kathy shrugged. "The great White Wolf."

"Oh. That sounds quite amazing." And lovely and normal.

"It was." This Kathy was a lot more chatty and a lot less judgey than the Kathy Paige had met the day before. "She helped me to understand the bond I needed to make between me and my wolf. It was very helpful."

"I don't think I was there to be helped."

Kathy turned to look at her. "What you mean?"

What Paige really needed was a human being to talk to.

What she really needed was her sister. But Kathy was just going to have to do. "I think I was there to be judged."

Kathy's eyebrows rose and she turned her attention back to the road.

"When Cawli found me, I thought he was there to help me. He was the answer to my prayers. I had this gaping hole to Hell inside my chest and I had no way to control it. I was like a bomb ready to go off. And he somehow knew to bind himself to me to fix that. I didn't ask any questions."

"And now you're wondering if maybe you should have?" Kathy's tone changed.

"Yeah. But not in the way you're thinking."

Kathy frowned at her. "Then how?"

Paige watched the horizon. "I think I'm being used."

"By who?"

Did she even want to admit this out loud? "By Cawli."

"That doesn't even make sense."

"I know. And that's what worries me."

"Then, what do you mean?"

It wasn't necessarily that she felt upset about being betrayed. Because in Paige's life, this one betrayal wasn't that horrible. "It worries me. If Cawli felt he needed to play this particular hand," Paige said turning her attention toward Kathy, "I'm afraid to see what's coming."

Kathy licked her lips and wrung the steering well with her hands. "Then it's true. He's invited the ancients back."

"You knew?"

"Why do you think we were so concerned? Is not just about the witches. We know about the Whiskeys. We know you're pretty decent as far as witches go. We're not super concerned about what you mean to our world."

"Well, I really wish that someone had clued me in before I stepped into this."

"Would you have done anything different?"

Paige thought about that for a long hard moment. "Probably not. I was desperate."

"Makes you wonder."

Paige turned to her. "Wonder what?"

"If maybe that was the reason. The reason for putting the door to Hell inside your soul. Maybe your demon *wanted* the ancients out."

A thread of dread ran down Paige's back. "That's a terrifying thought." Because if Sven had known, if he'd masterminded this...

"There isn't a single thing about any of this that makes any of us happy."

Paige shook her head not knowing what to do. Leslie was her sister and she needed this.

"Well then, you better pay attention to the next few days. Because what we're putting you through will determine whether you succeed or not."

"And if I don't? What's the threat?"

Kathy glanced at Paige out of the corner of her eye. "I don't need to threaten you. What you invited in will destroy you."

That was one thing that would never happen.

Leslie would *never* hurt her.

But what if the creature who had chosen her could?

EIGHT

WHEN THEY PULLED up to Doe's house, Paige's mind was running a mile a minute. Just how bad was this?

Kathy got out of the car.

Paige sat there for a long moment. She needed time. She needed to process.

What did Leslie need? Paige had no idea.

But sitting there thinking about it wasn't going to help anyone. She opened the door and got out.

She found Kathy in the living room with four others.

Paige knew that each one of these people was an alpha. She *knew* it. It was like an irritating itch at the back of her neck. When alphas were in the same room, they had an instinctive drive to challenge.

Paige wasn't feeling that. Was this new development? If so, was this development in the right direction?

Doe looked up at her and smiled, setting her mug down on the table in front of her. "I see you survived."

"I did."

Doe nodded once and gestured toward Kathy. "You managed to get your first vote."

"Are we still even looking for votes?"

Doe frowned. "What you mean?"

Paige looked to Kathy.

Kathy shrugged and gestured toward the group before disappearing into another room.

Well, there was nothing for it. "I know why I'm really here."

Doe folded her hands in front of her lap. "Is that so?"

Paige took in a deep breath. "The ancients are coming."

The two shifters on the couch resettled their weight uncomfortably. The shifter in the chair next to Doe remained still.

"Cawli invited them in."

Doe appeared pleased with the answers so far. "Yes, he did."

Paige noted that Doe hadn't asked who Cawli was.

Kathy reappeared from the kitchen with a tray of sandwiches. "*Who* did you see in the spirit cave?"

Paige'd forgotten that she hadn't actually told her. "Uh, the mammoth."

The two shifters on the couch exclaimed and muttered something under their breaths to one another. They may have been husband and wife. Paige just didn't know.

But the shifter in the leather chair to Doe's right still hadn't moved, his dark eyes never moving from Paige.

Doe grimaced. "And what did the mammoth say?"

Paige realized she should probably lie, but she just wasn't good at it. Her stomach rumbled loudly and she reached for a sandwich, wolfing it down between words. "He told me he didn't agree that the Whiskeys should have been brought in. He told me that a lot of trust had been given to us, and he told us not to screw up."

Doe blinked. "So, what are you going to do?"

Paige reached for another sandwich, not quite sure why she was so ravenous. "I don't know." And she didn't. "Did anyone else want one?"

"They're for you," Kathy said. "You were in there a few days."

A few...well, that certainly explained her hunger.

Doe met her gaze. "What do you want to do?"

That was simple. Paige chewed and swallowed carefully because she had nearly half a sandwich in her mouth. "I want to keep as many people safe as I can."

"And if that means killing one of your family because the ancient is out of control?"

Yeah. She wasn't killing Leslie. "I will do everything in my power to help her."

"Her." It wasn't a question.

"Yes." Paige didn't know if telling Doe this vital piece of information might endanger Leslie's life, but right now, Paige needed all the help she could get. "My sister."

The male shifter on the couch leaned back and rubbed his temple.

The female next to him leaned forward, resting her chin on her pointed fingers. "You know this for certain?"

Paige finished off her sandwich and waited for them to settle before grabbing another. "She was bitten by a child at the school. No one thought anything of it. However, Cawli said that an ancient chose her."

"How long ago was this?" Doe asked

"Months ago."

The shifter in the chair looked over at Doe, his expression grim.

Doe gave him an expression as if she was answering him. "Do you know who chose her?"

"No. Only that the ancient is very powerful. Chuck is

concerned. He can feel the power rising in his pack, and he knows he needs more to—" Paige shrugged because it didn't quite make sense.

"To help sponge the effects." Doe dropped her gaze in thought. "The situation is what we expected."

"Really?" Paige raised her hands to her sides and then slapped her hands down against her thighs, releasing her frustration. "Because *none* of this was expected."

Kathy sighed. "It appears as though Paige's been played just as much as the rest of us."

The man on the chair finally spoke. "How desperate was she to make this happen?"

Time to keep it honest. "Extremely. Someone had kidnapped me and branded the door to Hell inside my soul. I'm the demon summoner, so demons are kind of my job and every time I got near one, they possessed me and gained control of the door to Hell. So, yeah. I was pretty fucking desperate."

The woman on the couch dropped her hands. "What does that even mean?"

Paige turned toward her. "I'm going to let your imagination take that one."

Doe frowned and held up a hand to stop the man in the chair. "You still gained one vote today."

It was time for Paige to frown. She hadn't even entered into any of the trials yet. "I don't understand."

Doe gestured to Kathy. "Whatever you said, Kathy's with you."

"Thank you." Paige met Kathy's gaze and nodded once. She really did appreciate it.

Doe reached over and poured water from the China kettle into an empty cup. Then she took a teabag that was already prepared, and dumped it in. She handed it to Paige.

"You need some rest. It's been two days, and I doubt you've had any sleep."

Paige took the teacup and then sat in the chair on the other side of the coffee table. "I would rather get through these trials as quickly as I can. I really don't know what's waiting for me at home."

"You won't make it through any of the rest of the trials if you're exhausted."

She had a point. Paige sipped her tea. "A little rest couldn't hurt."

Doe sat down and picked up her own cup, sipping in silence.

The silence probably should have been awkward, but it just let Paige think and she appreciated that. There were too many things she still didn't know. Didn't understand. And it frustrated her that Cawli still wasn't trusting her with all of his information. Why bring the ancients out now? What was the point? Because they were needed?

Or because it was safe? "What do we really know about the ancients?"

The man in the chair narrowed his eyes and leaned forward. "What do you mean?"

Paige took another sip of her tea. It really did taste good. "I mean, I've been looking at this thinking that the ancients coming just meant that a terrible bad is on its way. When one power rises an equal and opposite power rises to balance it."

"What would make you think that?" Doe asked.

"It's just a balancing of power." And Paige didn't even understand if this was just a belief of hers, or if this was a real thing. "It's just something I've always believed. Like if you experience a run of really bad luck, then you just know that good luck is coming your way. That kind of thing. And so I'm concerned. The Whiskeys...we're gaining power and that worries me."

The woman on the couch turned toward Paige. "Enlighten us please."

Paige set her teacup on the saucer and set it on her lap, relaxing into the chair. "I mean that Leslie's children came into their gifts very early, very powerful. Her youngest was able to speak to people's minds straight out of the womb. Her middle son, Tyler, came into his gift very early as well."

"What does he do?"

"He's a bard."

The man in the chair frowned. "That doesn't sound terrible."

"Normally I would agree with you, but his voice is a force to be reckoned with. He can alter moods, thoughts, perceptions all with his voice." Paige blinked staring into her tea, everything relaxing, her mind letting go. "I'm just very concerned."

The man's expression grew fierce. "I would think you would rejoice. It means that your coven is very strong."

"It means," Paige said, letting her head fall back and her eyes close, "that something big is coming that needs all of us to be stronger sooner." She yawned. "And that scares me."

She didn't even realize that she had fallen asleep in the chair until a bright blue and white light woke her. She startled awake, and the tea cup and saucer crashed to the wood floor at her feet. Tea spilled across her toes, cold now as if it'd been sitting there for hours.

Paige turned around trying to find the source of the white light. It streamed through the window from the outside. It could have almost been a set of headlights, except that it didn't feel like it.

The room was empty. The furniture was still there, and

the cups remained on the table as though the shifters had just gotten up and walked out, leaving everything behind. Paige walked around to the front door and opened it peering outside.

The white light shined from a single source. Paige blinked, trying to figure out what it was that she was even seeing.

Standing in front of Kathy's car, stood a tall woman with the legs of a human, the bust of a woman, and the wings and head of a bird. The wings were white and lined with blue. It almost reminded her of the Native American totems she'd seen in some of the gift shops and stuff. What had those represented? She couldn't quite remember.

And standing beside her was a lion whose mane, tail, and paws were on fire.

What the heck was this? Paige walked down the steps. "Is this a trial?"

The woman stepped forward and the bird head dispersed into that of a human face, but the white and blue wings didn't disappear. If anything, they grew more powerful. Electricity danced along each feather. "No. We are not a trial."

Something inside Paige pulled her towards this woman and this lion who she knew was a man. She knew nothing about these two, but something made her trust them.

Love them.

"Do I know you?"

The woman smiled and gestured toward the lion. "Not yet."

The lion rose on his haunches, which morphed into human legs, his human feet still on fire. His front legs shifted into arms, flames dancing along his fingers. And his lion face morphed into a human face so very similar to the woman's, but his hair remained enflamed.

Paige had a suspicion. "I don't understand. What's going on?"

"We are your children."

Paige looked first to the girl and then to the boy. "What was in that tea?"

The girl smiled. "I don't know. But we're safe."

"You're trying to tell me," Paige said quietly, trying to wrap her head around what was happening, "that the animal spirits have already chosen you?"

"Yes." The girl turned toward her brother. "We haven't seen the sun and the rain in this realm for a very long time. And so, when we discovered you were pregnant, it was with great joy we discovered we were good match."

"A good match?"

"Yes."

It was obvious Paige wasn't getting any more information on that. "What are you?"

The girl took in a steadying breath and met Paige's gaze. "I am a thunderbird and my brother is a rajasi."

The words had been spoken almost as if in challenge. However, Paige really didn't know that much about either one. "Do you know if a great danger is coming our way?"

"I certainly hope not," the girl said softly. "Cawli said it was safe for us to come out now."

"Safe?"

"Yes. He said you and your family are capable of protecting us."

Seriously? "Why weren't you allowed to come out before?"

"We are very powerful," the boy said, his voice low and rumbly. "We are the protectors of the animal spirit realm."

"And?"

"And if our hosts are not strong enough," said the girl, "then we become a danger to the spirit animals we are sworn to protect."

That didn't sound amazing.

"It was good meet you, Mother."

A cold hand landed on Paige's arm. She jerked awake and the teacup fell, crashing against the wood floor, spilling warm liquid across her bare toes.

The man who had been sitting in the chair now stood over her, his dark eyes unreadable as he stared down at her.

So, all of that had been a vision?

The man turned toward Doe and nodded. Then he left, slamming the door behind him.

Doe looked up and met Paige's gaze. "It appears you've gained another vote."

Votes were good. Except that what she was learning was only making her more terrified.

NINE

WHEN PAIGE WOKE UP, she discovered about a dozen messages from Michelle, Rainbow, Ethel, and Tuck.

Tuck had left actual voice messages. Chuck had as well.

None, however, from Dexx.

She called Michelle first. "Whiskey. What's up?"

Michelle released a pent-up breath of frustration. "Rainbow's been arrested."

Wait. "What?" Paige sat up straight in bed. "Tell me what's going on?"

Apparently, it looked like Rainbow had released a man they'd had in lockup and had killed him down by the river. They had video surveillance and everything.

Dexx's name had even been *carved* onto the body.

"We're being framed," Michelle said. "It's bigger than just Rainbow. She was just the easiest. Dexx knows it. We all do. We need you."

"I'll be there as soon as I can," Paige said, knowing that might be a day, a week. She just didn't know.

"Get here now."

Paige hung up with Michelle and immediately called Dexx. "What's going on over there?"

Dexx sounded cheerful and upbeat. "It's being handled."

Which was his way of saying—what? She didn't even know. It could mean that everything was fine, but it could mean he'd dumped gas in the trash can and had the lit matches in his hands while they spoke.

"I've got the situation under control. It's good here. Like, all good. How are you?"

She couldn't believe him. She *loved* him, but *trusted* Michelle. "I see what you're trying to do. You can't *Han Solo* out of it. They said a body had your name carved it. Why?"

He didn't answer right away, which meant he was actually thinking about his reply.

This was so bad.

"Barn's got the autopsy. If there's something to find, he will."

Great. "Tell me this isn't Sven."

"It might be."

At least he wasn't trying to cover *that* part up. Doe and her pack be damned. Paige had to hope the alpha had learned enough for Paige to relieve herself of these trials. "I'm coming home."

After a brief conversation that spanned several different topics including socks and boxes and love bodies, she hung up the phone convinced she needed to go back. Spirit caves were nothing compared to murder convictions.

The smell of food filled the air, tempting Paige. She freshened up and returned downstairs, intent on telling them she had to leave. Right after she fed herself and her two starving unborn children.

Doe looked up from the stove. "I was worried. I didn't know how long you would sleep."

"I guess I was more tired than I thought." Which should have her concerned. She'd never slept this long while pregnant before, though she'd been a lot *younger* the first time. "Three days? Really?"

Doe turned back to the stove with a nod. "Pregnancy will do that to you. You've gotta be careful about how hard you push yourself now."

Which brought her directly to the point. Paige closed her eyes, regretting what she was about to say, but so many emotions washed over her, the words were almost forced out. "I can't stay."

"You have to." Doe gave her a frank yet understanding look.

"My team is in trouble."

"You need to learn to trust them." Doe stirred whatever was in the cast iron skillet. "*You* aren't needed. *They* don't need you. You feel the need to be there to control the situation."

She might be right most of the time, but they needed her *this* time. "Sven is closing in on my team. He's framing one of them for murder."

"Then we should hurry."

Paige couldn't believe Doe was being so unmovable. "I don't think you're understanding the gravity of the situation. Sven is powerful and somehow he just gets even *more* powerful. None of us know how or why. My team is in *prison* right now. They're being *framed* for murder."

Doe didn't look apologetic. "That sounds bad, but you've got responsibilities of your own. They're here."

"No." Paige grabbed a roll off the plate Doe offered her and shoved practically the whole thing in her mouth. It wasn't what she wanted. She needed protein, but the roll would tide her over for now. "You don't understand. My *responsibility* is to my team and my family. Not to yours."

The corners of Doe's mouth drooped as she turned away. "That's not true."

"I assure you it is."

"Nope." Doe put a lid on a pot on the stove and turned back to her. "Whatever you *were* before all this is changed now. You were a detective, right?"

Paige nodded. "And now I run a—"

"Give it to someone else."

"You don't under—"

"You don't," Doe roared, her alpha will flaring. "You're a shifter witch now. The *power* in your control is your responsibility. How it affects your family is your responsibility. How it affects your pack, your town, your region? That's your responsibility. Solving murders is not."

Paige fumbled through the forest of thoughts those words invoked. "Who are you protecting?"

Doe swallowed hard, then shook her head and grabbed a bowl, filling it with what looked like stew. "We need to know if we can trust you."

Paige took the bowl, trying to ignore the insatiable hunger filling her. "Not because you're going to fight beside me when Sven comes to call. Not because you want me to fight beside you if some enemy comes to your door."

"That *is* why packs align."

It was time to get to the point. "It's because you need to know if you can trust the shifter witch you have."

Doe's expression didn't change.

Right on the money.

"Eat. The next challenge could drain you."

An hour and several helpings of stew later, Paige made

up her mind. She and Dexx would find another way to help Leslie and their unborn children. Her *team* needed her *now*.

Paige squared off with Doe. "You need to figure out how to help your shifter witch on your own and stop using it as an excuse to stay out of Chuck's pack. We both know that isn't what's really going on here."

Doe rubbed her head. "You're really choosing your team over the safety of your pack."

"I'll find a way to help both."

Doe narrowed her eyes but said nothing else except to make arrangements for Paige to get to the airport.

Paige didn't call Chuck or anyone else to let them know she was coming home. She didn't want to give anyone the heads up and she definitely didn't want to get an earful from Chuck. Instead, she flew under the radar, rented a car, to meet Dexx at home.

When he finally showed up an hour later, he was wet and naked. Well the robe covered him, but he was naked under it.

They sat on the couch together and talked with Leslie and Tru. Paige waited to hear about the horrors that were happening. She didn't doubt Leslie knew all about it. After all, Barn was doing the autopsies and he worked with her part-time.

But no one said anything.

Dexx played everything cool as a cucumber, which wasn't helping her trust him. She understood he might be trying to shield her from his issues, thinking he had it under control, but she just didn't believe it. Yes. She had her own issues—her growing power and her pregnancy with powerful unborn children was only one of them. But they were supposed to be partners, first, and she was his boss second.

She finally told him she knew what was going on and he just got upset that Michelle had told her, like she'd betrayed his trust. When Paige offered her assistance, he just asked how the budget was going with his ten thousand dollar dead guy. The ten thousand dollars was the damage Dexx had made to the town of Troutdale while apprehending the now dead prisoner.

Yeah. Things were *bad*.

But if the man wasn't going to use *her* as a partner, she'd use him. "I'm pregnant."

The look on his face said he was surprised but mildly terrified. "Have you taken a test?"

"Didn't really need to. Apparently, shifters can just smell it on me."

"Why didn't you find out, before... before..."

"Before what?" Paige didn't know what was going on inside *his* head, but she knew what was happening inside hers. He was afraid of these kids, too. "Before I'm attacked at the trials which I've failed now, by the way? Or before Sven starts a war? Or before you decide maybe you don't want to be a dad?"

"No, not that. I don't know—"

"Maybe *you* need to figure out what *you* want." Paige couldn't believe this was going down this way. Dexx was such a great dad to Leah and Bobby. She hadn't *actually* thought he'd...

Would he leave?

"I think." Dexx puffed out his cheeks and released a long breath. "I think we'll be the best parents a magickal, broom-riding little bundle of joy could have." He reached around her and pulled her in tight.

That was a sudden shift in emotion. "So, you aren't scared?"

"Nope. Not scared. I'm *terrified*." He tucked her head to his chest. "With the danger, we bring to our kids—"

Oh. That. "I know," she said relieved. "What are we thinking?"

"But if Leslie and Tru can have a whole bunch of kids without killing them, then we can, too. And we come with babysitters and everything already built in."

She'd just dumped the fact they were having *a* baby on him. She didn't want to inform him they were having twins *or* that she already knew the animal spirits who had chosen them. The best way to give Dexx information was a little bit at a time. "Yeah, babysitters."

Dexx fell to the bed. "We're gonna be fine."

No. She was pretty sure they wouldn't be.

She then spent the next two days attempting to help her team get out from under the murder charges just like Tuck had demanded.

Chuck was livid with her. He'd met her on the sidewalk briefly. He hadn't said a single word. He'd just stared at her real hard and then spun on his heel and left.

Paige knew Doe needed her, but—that was the thing. Doe didn't need *her*. Doe needed Paige to *show* her that everything would be okay with her own shifter witch, whoever the poor witch was.

But Paige didn't know if that was possible.

She *did* try to shift a few times on her own. She'd brought Leah along with her as a gal-pal. She knew kids weren't supposed to be "pals" to their parents, but she'd wanted *someone* to be there with her when she tried to shift for the first time. Cawli was absolutely no help and she didn't want to bother Dexx with this. Chuck was still very mad at her, so that was no help. So, Leah—for all that she was a tween-aged necromancer—was her best bet.

She'd surprisingly had a few good clues and tips and tricks. Her best friend was a horse shifter and this was something they'd apparently discussed at great length. Leah wanted to be a shifter because her witch powers sucked. She theorized that when a witch was bitten, her powers were turned off and replaced by the shifting ability.

Paige wasn't about to tell her that wasn't true because there was a good chance Leah *might* be bitten sometime. They hadn't thought Leslie would be, after all.

But even with the tips and tricks, Paige hadn't been able to shift. She finally gave up, realizing that maybe shifting just wasn't for her.

She kept her eyes on Leslie, but aside from her and Tru giving her and Dexx a hard time about the pregnancy, Leslie seemed normal. Dexx didn't seem out of balance. The pack seemed fine.

Maybe everyone was overreacting.

Paige leaned against the porch post staring across the property. People *had* to be overreacting. But if they weren't...

Chuck slipped out of the woods surrounding the Whiskey house in his black wolf form and stopped in front of Paige for a long, stony moment.

Paige winced. She realized this conversation had to be coming. "You might as well shift." She reached over to the robe hutch and pulled out the one on top, offering it to him.

He shifted into a deliciously naked man and took the robe from her, slipping it on. "Doe is willing to restart the trials."

"I'm not." Paige wasn't leaving her team. That wasn't going to happen.

"Leslie needs this."

"Right." Paige was tired of hearing the lame excuse. "I don't think so. What's really going on?"

Chuck narrowed his Caribbean blue eyes. "Exactly what I said."

"And?"

His eyes narrowed to slits. "And," he growled, his alpha will rising, "Doe has a shifter witch in her pack. She's having a similar issue I am, though hers isn't as powerful."

"As Leslie's? As me *and* Leslie *and* the twins?"

"Twins?" Chuck asked, the edge of his anger turning slightly.

She nodded, not knowing what else to say except, "I haven't told Dexx yet."

He closed his eyes for a moment, then opened them. "In that case, we most definitely need Doe's pack."

"And..." No. She was *needed* here. "What happens if I don't?"

Chuck's released breath was shaky. "We could lose control of the entire pack. Her spirit or the spirits of your children might very well rise up and destroy us. We just don't know. The spirits you have are—"

"Ancients," Paige finished for him.

His mouth fell open slightly in surprise. "They were erased from the world for a reason."

"Cawli said it was safe for them."

"He was wrong." Chuck shook his head. "It is not safe."

"It's too late. Unless you can get Leslie's spirit animal to back off? They haven't bonded fully or whatever because that's still quiet. Right? And my kids? They're still in the womb. Maybe he can talk to the thunderbird and tell her to leave my little girl alone."

"Thund—girl?" Chuck frowned and clamped his lips shut. "You talked to the seer. She showed you."

She shrugged and shook her head. "Sure. I guess?"

"And what is the other one?"

"He's a…" What was the name again? "Rajasi?"

Chuck's expression was blank and then his eyes widened in alarm. "We need Doe's pack."

That bad? "She wouldn't let me back in again if I went back groveling, which I'm not because *I'm needed here.*"

"But have you actually accomplished anything?"

No. She hadn't, but she was still digging into it. Sometimes, it took a moment to get things moving.

"Trust Dexx to manage this without you. Go back to Doe. Start the trials again."

This went against everything Paige felt was important. "We can figure out a different solution."

"No," Chuck said firmly. "We cannot."

Paige *hated* this. "She won't let me."

"Oh, but she will."

It was time for Paige to narrow her eyes. "Her shifter witch."

"He's not as powerful, but he *is* putting a drain on her pack."

"And you think that adding her pack *and* her shifter witch is *still* going to help yours?"

Chuck nodded.

"And it'll help Leslie?"

He kept nodding.

"And the little ones?" Who needed names.

He didn't stop.

Fuck. She looked away, not looking forward to her next conversation with Dexx. But the truth was, Dexx *was* handling the Red Star situation pretty well on his own. And she *hadn't* been able to get anything major accomplished, though she'd managed to put a *few* things in motion that would probably help. Leah and Bobby were fine. Leslie was okay for now.

"You'll keep an eye on Les?" she asked without realizing she'd voiced the question.

"Always," he said quietly. "She *is* mine."

When *he* said that, a true alpha, she felt it meant *more* than him simply claiming her to belong to him. He had also given himself to her.

Paige couldn't throw *that* away. "Fine. What do I need to do?"

TEN

SHE NEEDED TO GROVEL.

Paige arrived *back* in Utah the next day and was ignored for a day and a half. She'd lost one of her votes by leaving—Kathy—and she'd had to work hard to talk herself back into Kathy's good graces.

She still wasn't there.

On day three of being back, Paige had received few updates from Troutdale, only a pointed message from Chuck to pay attention and focus. Not knowing how the investigation was progressing wasn't helping her do that.

Paige stepped into the kitchen, her nose leading the way. "What do you need from me, Doe? You need to protect your shifter witch. I need to protect mine. So...how do we do that?"

Doe stood at the stove again, this time with a large cast iron flat pan. "How do I know you're not going to simply leave again as soon as the trials start back up?"

Paige had that coming. "You told me to trust my team. I—" She needed to put less "I" and her statement and more "pack." But what did Doe need to hear? "If we fail at Red Star, we fail the entire town. I lead that."

"Let someone else," Doe ground out.

"I'm not a leader of any pack. I'm not an alpha."

"You are."

Paige didn't even really know what that meant. "Dexx is the alpha of our pack."

"There are two alphas of your pack. Dexx is only one half of your mated pair."

Paige bared her teeth in frustration and paced away. She stopped, the smell of cooking meat making her stomach do flipflops. "What do *you* need from me in regards to your own shifter witch?"

Doe was quiet for a long moment, preparing whatever they were having for dinner. Finally, she spoke. "I need to know if he can remain with us, if we should turn him out, or if we need to kill him."

Whoa. "Kill hi—Doe. You're serious."

Doe nodded silently.

"The stories are just stories."

"They are not. I can assure you there *is* legitimacy to th—" She turned to Paige, spoon in hand. "I saw with my own eyes as a shifter witch tore through our entire pack when I was very young. He was stronger, faster, harder to harm or kill. But he lacked magick. Something—" Doe licked her lips. "Ours—now—still has magick."

This one was chosen, Cawli growled low in Paige's mind. *The other stole his spirit animal.*

Paige didn't realize that was a thing. "You're really going to kill him?"

"If I must? My pack comes first, as should yours. If your shifter witches—" She glanced at Paige's belly and then back up to her face. "—threaten the lives of your pack, you *must* deal with them."

Paige shook her head. "But what if we're not as bad as you think?"

"Then," Doe said, a thread of hope lighting her expression, "he gets to live. As does your sister, your babes, and yourself."

Paige pressed her thumb between her eyes and chanted for patience. "What do you need me to do?"

"Take the next trials seriously."

Paige raised both hands in an open gesture. "Okay."

Doe raised her chin and turned back to the stove. "The trial is very simple. Capture that flag—" She pointed to the flag on top of a hill Paige could barely see through the window. "—and put it on your tower before the other team does."

"Awesome." Paige released a long sigh and headed to the back door. This was not going to end well.

Cawli coiled in anticipation, almost feeling excited.

At least one of them was. "And who's my team?"

"Those who haven't voted for you yet."

That...didn't make much sense. "So, everyone? Who are we opposed?"

A woman stepped up to them from the side of the house as if she'd been summoned and held out her hand.

Paige stepped out of the house and offered her own.

This was the woman who'd been on the couch. "Jean Little," she said. "I'm Lyle's wife." Her brown hair was swept back in a loose braid, and her green eyes shown brightly.

Paige liked her almost immediately.

Lyle stepped up beside his wife and offered his hand, his brown hair tied up in a manbun, his dark eyes penetrating. "Nice to meet you. This must be interesting for you, I'd bet."

Paige took his hand as well. Neither of them had tried to overpower her, which was pleasant and a little refreshing. "You have no idea."

"Oh, I do." Jean gave her a tight smile. "I'm a seer who was bitten and they put me through the same paces."

A seer? So, was *she* the one who'd put the vision whammy on her? "I didn't realize there were problems with seers trying to entrap shifters."

Jean's eyes widened. "Maybe not that, but lead them astray? Trick them? Cheat them?" She nodded. "I thought that having been chosen by a spirit would be enough to get them to trust me."

Humans lack in trust, Cawli said in Paige's mind.

She didn't need to be told that one. She already knew it. "Well, then I'm glad you're on my team?" Because she wasn't sure.

Lyle shrugged. "I'm not convinced you're good for our community."

"Neither am I."

He frowned.

Paige shrugged, shaking her head. "Keeping it honest. The more I learn about what I am and how I got to be here, the more concerned I become."

Lyle straightened, watching her through narrowed eyes. "That makes me feel a little better."

"I'm glad it does one of us." Because it didn't for her. At all. "So, what's the plan?"

Jean turned and pointed to another man behind her. "That's Wade and his mate Erica. They have the local coyote pack, and they are definitely not with you."

"Great."

"Yeah. Anyway, they're the strongest alphas we have."

And Paige needed to win while playing nice and not losing control of her very powerful magick. This was going to be great. "Okay, so..."

Jean held up her hands. "Just follow his lead."

"I'm not really good with that," Paige said, stepping off the back porch—in her tennis shoes she'd almost left in Oregon—and leading the way towards the other alpha pair.

"This should be interesting then," Lyle said, a chuckle almost recognizable in his voice.

Wade glared at Paige when she came to stand by him. He was tall, probably taller than Chuck, and ginger as all get-out. He was freckled, his red hair curly and unruly. However, he made it look impressive.

Paige held out her hand. "Paige Whiskey."

He ignored her hand.

She wanted to roll her eyes at the man but offered her hand toward the woman. "Pleasure to meet you."

The woman narrowed her green eyes, her wild red hair pulled back in a loose ponytail at the nape of her neck. "Erica. That one is Wade."

Erica *did* try the overpowering handshake. She squeezed. Hard.

Paige smiled tightly and squeezed back.

Cawli crept forward and added a bit of his power into the squeeze.

Erica raised an eyebrow, but released her grip and stepped closer to her husband. The woman looked petite next to him.

"I was informed what our objective is," Paige said, trying to peer through the orchard to the hill that hid behind the trees from this angle. "What's the plan?"

Wade studied her for a long moment, and then turned away. "They have traps laid out between us and the hill."

"We have a few of our own," Jean added.

"Sounds fair." What the hell were they doing? Trying to kill each other? "How well were we able to keep booby traps away from our tower?"

"Probably as well as they were." Lyle grinned. "There were a few I'm willing to bet they didn't find."

"Which means," Paige said, "there are probably a few missed on our side as well."

Wade's ginger eyebrows flicked. "Probably."

"Plan?"

Wade stared at the orchard trees. "I want you sidelined."

"I get that." And she did. "But that kind of defeats the purpose of this trial."

"It does."

"So." Paige clasped her hands behind her back. "Plan." How was she able to remain so calm and in control of herself when surrounded by so many alphas? Normally, being around just one set her on edge. Well, everyone except Dexx.

Erica pointed with her chin. "You, me, and Jean go to the hill. Meanwhile, Wade and Lyle go to our tower and try to find any boobytraps that weren't taken care of. And then protect it."

"How serious do these things get?"

"What are you asking?" Erica's gaze was pointed like a knife.

"I'm asking, how worried for my life should I be? Should I be in fighting-demons mode, or should I be in flag-football mode?"

Wade drummed his fingertips against his thigh. "We are not playing flag football."

Great. And it would probably be frowned on if she used her witch abilities.

You use whatever abilities you have in your arsenal, kitten, Cawli said.

Kitten? That was the first time he'd ever been so informal. "Okay. When do we start?"

Wade motioned to Doe.

Kathy waved from the other side of the yard.

Doe nodded to both of them. She raised a red flag over her head and then let it drop.

Jean led the way through the orchard trees, running as if running was something everyone did all the time.

Blessed Mother, Paige needed to get in shape.

Erica ran after Jean without a thought.

Wade and Lyle took off toward the tower.

Taking in her last deep breath she was likely to breathe for the rest of the day, Paige took off after to the two women.

But after several feet, she was *still* breathing easy, instead of ready to lose half a lung. Nice.

She could feel Cawli in the back of her mind, in her legs, her arms. Was this what it felt like to be a shifter? She didn't want to jinx it, so she kept her thoughts to herself. Instead, she called the air as they ran to search for boobytraps in front of them.

Erica came to a sudden stop and turned on Paige. "What are you doing?"

Paige stopped, scanning the area with her eyes. "What do you mean?"

"You're doing something with the air."

Oh, for crying out loud. "I'm a witch, Erica. I asked the air to scout ahead and let us know—" The air tugged on her hair and pointed her attention to a scarecrow in the middle of the orchard.

Jean jogged back toward them. "What's going on?"

An image of falling tree limbs entered Paige's mind. Air wasn't a great communicator. "There's a boobytrap at the scarecrow."

Erica narrowed her green eyes, her red hair dancing wildly in the breeze. "What?"

"I can ask the air to do things, but it's not great at giving me specifics." The smell of churned wood tickled her nose. "Something to do with fire and falling sticks."

"In the orchard."

Paige shrugged.

Jean gestured to the right. "Then we go around. Come on."

They ran like that, Paige letting them know when they were about to come up on a boobytrap before they got to it. Well, if the air could see it as a bad thing so that meant a few were missed.

Jean was whacked pretty hard with a log once, but she was doing okay.

Erica was starting to turn her opinion, or at least Paige was pretty sure. There was a lot less judgement and a lot more working together. Within twenty minutes, they had the flag in their possession and were running back toward their tower.

The air hit Paige in the face and a growl filled her right ear. She held out her arm, stopping Jean. "Ambush," she said quietly.

Jean gestured to Erica. They both crouched.

"How dangerous is this going to get?" Paige asked. She knew herself by now. When her back was against a wall, her magick tended to protect her pretty well, but that was before she was pregnant. She didn't want to get into a position where she was forced to act.

"Don't kill anyone, but fight like they're intending to end you." Jean raised her nose to the wind, and then gestured to the left.

Great.

Erica and Paige followed.

"Know where they are?" Erica asked quietly.

Paige gestured to the right. She raised her nose to the air and sniffed. She could feel two energy patterns almost as if they were electric wires buzzing with current. She held up two fingers.

Erica nodded and dashed quietly into the undergrowth.

Jean gestured for Paige to circle around.

Before she had a chance, she was attacked by a large, broad wolf. His teeth clamped onto her arm, dragging her to the ground.

Cawli growled low, power building in her legs.

Paige pushed the wolf away, sending him into a cherry tree.

He yipped but got back to his feet.

Another wolf joined them.

Paige grinned, Cawli curling in excitement, electricity and fire running through her veins.

The grey wolf leapt at her.

She crouched, prepared to protect herself—

And then blinding pain split her skull.

Attack.

The wards around the Whiskey home shouted inside her skull, demanding power, commanding strength.

Paige's power rose inside her, answering the call. The Whiskey wards were a part of her, tied to her very soul, like the demon door, but unlike it, she'd given her soul to feed those wards freely, fueling them with love.

She stopped and closed her hands into fists. She didn't know *how* to send magick to them. She was in Utah. Those wards were in Oregon.

A vision of blazing white rivers of magick floated up to her mind's eye.

Ley lines.

Except witches couldn't *access* those.

But her earth magick could. Her fire magick could. Her air and water magick could. All four of them together could.

Her life magick could.

One of those magicks wouldn't touch the ley lines with a great deal of power or effect. That was something she gleaned from the image from whoever or whatever was giving it to her. But with all five elements, all five magicks?

But could she send that power safely?

The answer was confusion. The element sending her this information didn't understand "safe." It wouldn't be hurt.

Great.

Her home wards faltered and gasped.

She had to act now. Power built in Paige's fist. With a roar of *will* and a mindset of safety, she slammed it into the earth, pushing it with all the power of her heart toward her home and *away* from the people here, focusing on the natural veins of ley lines of the earth.

The power shot forward, finding the easiest path to the ley lines and then sped along it, leaving her to support her wards.

She'd done it.

A concussive wall of sound exploded away from her in a dome of spent magick.

Silence.

Rising to her feet, Paige looked around, shaking off the effects the wards, not looking forward to what she was going to find. *Sound* had escaped her, so those around her shouldn't be overly injured. Except her nephew was a bard and she *knew* just how dangerous sound could be. Damn it. *Cawli, what happened?*

You will have to call home to find out.

Fuck.

The two wolves who had been in the process of attacking lay on the ground motionless a few feet away. Leaves and flower petals littered the ground.

What the hell had she done? She'd *never* touched ley lines before. She was a *witch*. She *couldn't*. Was this her unborn children?

It is not, Cawli said quietly. *This was you.*

She pulled out her phone as she ran to the first wolf, unlocking the phone with her thumb pad. "Hey," she said to the wolf, putting her hand on the grey pelt. "You okay?"

The wolf didn't move, but he breathed.

This wasn't good. If Doe decided she was too powerful —if this other shifter witch was too powerful—then she'd just killed another person with this stunt.

What the *fuck* had attacked the house? And were her damned kids safe? Bobby? He was a damned baby with an ability to glow at people. Anger built inside her as she hit the green phone button on Dexx's number. It didn't go through. She had no reception.

Fuck.

She stashed her phone in her back pocket and turned her attention to the wolf. *Is he okay?*

Who? Cawli asked. *Dexx or the wolf?*

Both. *The wolf.*

He was stunned by your magick, but seems to be otherwise okay. It was a quite powerful force.

That...probably wasn't going to win her any points. *Do you know who he is?*

Lyle.

Paige winced. "Hey, Lyle." She rubbed his back. If she could show she didn't actually *hurt* anyone, she might be okay. "Come on back, buddy."

He whuffed a breath and opened his blue eyes.

She smiled at him. "Hey."

Seeing her, he scrambled to his paws and growled low.

Oh, great.

She held out her hands and took a step back. "Everything's okay. You're fine, right? Not dead?"

Lyle growled low again.

Paige crouch-walked toward the other prone wolf. *Who's this?*

Kathy.

Paige reached a hand and dug her fingers gently into Kathy's thick fur. "Hey, Kath, wake up."

Kathy stirred and then shot to her paws. After a moment, she went to Lyle's side and stood with him, staring at Paige.

Jean and Erica stood behind them.

Doe entered the area and assessed the situation. "I think we're done here."

Crap. Paige had to explain. She could read on everyone's faces and in Doe's tone that she'd lost. But it was more than that. There was a settled resolve in Doe's eyes. She was going to kill her shifter witch. "The house was attacked. I used a type of magick only I have."

"The house here was attacked?"

Did Doe just look right over the fact that she'd said she'd

used a magick only she had because the look in her eyes hadn't changed. "No, at home. My home. The wards started...screaming. It had to have been major." Doe wasn't getting it. "Okay. I deal with demons all the time and those wards have *never* acted like this. When I say it's major, I mean it's bigger than I *normally* deal with. I need to call them and see what happened and if they're okay."

Doe studied her for a long moment and then nodded. "We're done."

Here. Now. But she hadn't abandoned her family *again* to turned away after the first trial. Too many shifter witches relied on her. She'd get Doe to see this. "Everyone's okay?"

"Yeah." Doe turned back toward the house and set her hand on Paige's shoulder. "Except you just lost two votes."

Paige closed her eyes as the pack walked past her.

If Dexx wasn't dead, she was going to kill him.

ELEVEN

PAIGE DUCKED everyone's glares as she walked around the house and to the front. Pulling out her phone, she saw she had three bars and then tried Dexx again.

He picked up after the first ring. "Hey, baby, found reception, huh?"

She was going to take that calm sexy voice and punch him in the nuts. "Is everyone okay?"

"Sure, everything's fine."

He was playing it cool again. After something *major* had just happened? She was going to kill him.

"Why? Did you hear something?"

"I felt the wards." And then she'd exploded and shit.

He sighed.

"Something attacked." How could she convey over the phone just how *pissed* she was? "It was huge. What's going on there?"

"Uh." It sounded like he was stalling, trying to figure out how handle her, and that just pissed her off even more. "It was nothing, really."

Tarik chuckled in the background in a voice that wasn't entirely Tarik.

Dexx cleared his throat. "You remember Mike Jones? The angel?"

Paige wasn't about to forget him. He was the sick fuck who'd helped Sven open a gate to Hell inside Paige's soul, putting her in this damned situation in the first goddamned place.

Okay. Maybe she needed to calm down. That was a lot of curse words even for her.

She was pissed. "From St. Francisville? *What happened?*"

Dexx made a sound like he was caught between a rock and a bad place. "I was chased. He had a copy of Jackie. An *exact* copy."

Paige blinked. The wards had popped *that...damned... bad...*and he was *worried about his frelling car?*

"We ran around town, and I thought maybe that wasn't such a good idea because I *am* learning."

Thank the goddess for small miracles. He had a nasty habit of chasing people in town and breaking buildings.

"So, I ran him into the wards. Roadrunner style."

Paige breathed. She didn't know if she was able, but she was tempted to reach her witch hands through the phone and strangle him. "Dexx, I can't leave. Things are hanging by a thread here, and I left so I could get reception to call."

"I got this, babe. Don't worry. We even have a few leads we can work on. Time crunch and all."

"Human," Tarik said low.

Their djinn sounded possessed. She, the demon summoner, had the ability to send whatever was possessing him away, and she was stuck... playing capture the flag. "Dexx, I—" Don't kill him. Don't kill him. Don't kill him. "I love you. Be careful out there." Because she was going to kill him when she got back and that would be hard to do if he died *first*.

"I always am, Pea. Even when I'm reckless."

Really? He was going to give her *that*? "It's really Mike Jones?" The pounding in her skull was giving her a headache.

He paused. "Yup."

"He's dangerous. Too dangerous for you alone. I'm coming home." *To kill you. And then save you.*

Kitten, Cawli said quietly, a hint of mirth in his tone.

"He's only really dangerous to Jackie clones."

If he mentioned his car one more time. "I'm serious, Dexx."

"So am I." He *did* sound it...in Dexx-style. "I brought in Frey."

"Who?"

"Uh, Greta Van Sant. The Valkyrie."

Why would Dexx change her *name?* "I don't get the Frey thing."

"I wouldn't make a big deal about it, really. She likes it better. And why wouldn't she? Greta? Really? Even I'd rather be a Frey."

Paige took in a deep, steadying breath and slowly released it, trying to remind herself that he was focusing on the details that didn't matter because he was *handling* the details that *did*.

"Also, super handy in a demon fight."

"He's not a demon." He was an angel, which made him even worse.

"Also, super handy in an angel fight. She has a sword that disappears, babe. Like... it *disappears*."

Paige counted to ten.

"Trust me. I'll have this all wrapped up in a jiffy. "

"Please, Dexx. Be careful. He's an angel, remember?" And they didn't need an angel getting close to their God's prophet toddler. Bobby wasn't nearly as powerful as the other kids.

"Of course. I won't take unnecessary risks."

Did he *really* just say that? Out loud? "That's what I'm afraid of. I love you, and I'll be home as soon as the trial wraps up." Which... shouldn't be too much longer.

"You're a lawyer, now?"

She bit her tongue, reminding herself he was just being funny. "I love you. See you later."

"Knock 'em dead." The phone clicked.

She stashed her phone in her back pocket and ran her fingers through her hair. This was stupid. She was out in the middle of the damned desert playing games when Dexx was being chased by Mike freakin' Jones. He hadn't seemed as bad as Sven in St. Francisville, but she hadn't been quite in her right mind then, either.

But it pissed her off more that Dexx was more concerned with the "false Jackies" than the fact that their kids were attacked by a damned angel.

She needed to go home, which meant she needed to get this situation under control.

Paige stepped into the house, searching for Doe.

She knelt beside Lyle, talking to him quietly.

Taking in a deep breath, Paige stood beside them both. "We're under attack at home. I have to get back." Which meant she wanted to speed this along, but to do that, Paige needed the alpha to understand what they were up against. This was *more* than shifter witches and packs. This was *serious*.

Doe stood and turned to Paige. "You also need to rally support, to bring more packs to your region."

Paige wasn't arguing that. "It's an angel. And a really bad one."

"And if things are as bad as you say they are," Doe said, pointing a finger toward the ground, "then you need to gain the trust of the people here."

At this slow rate? She'd been on her way to gaining their trust and then that disappeared when she'd used more magick than she'd ever used before. Doe was going to *kill* her shifter witch. Because of Paige. This entire situation was stupid. "You don't understand," Paige shouted, anger curling in her belly.

Doe squared off with her. "Then *make* me understand."

She wanted to get what Paige was dealing with? Fine. "You're forcing me to hold your fucking hand while a powerful man is attacking my family. You're scared of a person who has magick and the ability to shift because one guy—one guy in your past—destroyed your pack. Because *all* shifter witches are the same? Probably not, but okay. Right now, my family—my kids—my toddler—is under attack. This guy was one of the people responsible for opening the gate to Hell inside my soul."

Doe shrugged. "So?"

So? *So?* "He's at my house attacking my kids." The force of Paige's will ripped toward the front, punctuating each word, filling it with the desperation she couldn't hide. "And my damned fool mate who's supposed to be protecting them is more worried about his *damned fucking car*."

Doe's eyes flashed and then something shifted in her expression.

A hand touched Paige's arm and calm flowed through her.

Jean stared up at her. "I doubt he's more worried about the car."

She must be an empath at some level. With the fuel of her anger dispelled, Paige was ready to dissolve into tears. "You've never met Dexx and his car."

Erica chuckled, remaining on the couch. "Maybe not Dexx, but we've met the type."

Why were they laughing?

Paige spun away, yanking her hair off her face, taking in a deep breath.

"You feel helpless," Doe said quietly.

Yeah. She did. "I'm in the wrong place."

"Maybe." Doe's tone didn't offer alternatives. "But we're not going to stop now."

Because Doe wanted to keep her shifter witch alive? Or because she wanted Paige to show her it was okay to kill her? "They're under attack as we speak. My son. My daugh—" She couldn't even finish that word through the thick haze of emotion. She'd fought so hard to get her daughter back only so she could endanger the girl's life?

"You have your own pack to protect your kids."

"They're no match against *angels*." Paige closed her eyes, her ears buzzing from the rush of emotion running through her.

"You also have a coven of witches."

Doe was right.

"He's still an angel and this one teams up with demons." Paige took in a calming breath, keeping her back toward the room. She wasn't an emotional person. Or, rather, she was. She just kept them battened down really well. "I'm worried."

"Be worried but stay in control." Doe's soft footsteps padded away.

Paige breathed in, calmer now, and turned back. "Is anyone hurt?"

"A few busted ribs." Erica shrugged. "All in all, not bad with as much power you had."

"I can... I can help the healing."

"We're shifters." Jean said quietly. "We heal quickly."

Paige knew that. "It'll make *me* feel better."

Erica chuckled and stepped out of the way. "Then, by all means."

Feeling the eyes of the alphas in the room, Paige walked forward and set her hands on Lyle's shoulder. She closed her eyes and called for the All Mother, singing the lullaby of love and nurturing, the call coming easier with her pregnancy. The pull of the earth was strong and came easily. Healing energies coursed through her, blooming from her womb and winding through her veins like a network of glowing strands of silk.

They reached toward Lyle, creeping up his neck and then down his chest, the tips wavering as if they were blood hounds on the scent.

Peace filled Paige as the energies found their mark.

And then pain lanced her ribs where Lyle's had been broken. The energy pulled from Paige's body, reminding Lyle's ribs what it was like to be whole. When the pain ebbed, the strands retreated, pulling back into her body, rolling around Paige's womb, and crept back toward the earth.

Paige opened her eyes, releasing a long, relaxed breath.

The room was silent.

Blood rushed to Paige's face, making her neck feel uncomfortably warm. "Should I not have?"

Erica shook her head, her eyes wide. "Lyle? You feel okay?"

He poked his own side and smiled, rising to his feet. "I haven't felt this good since before the accident. I might be back to brand new."

Paige frowned.

"He broke his ribs when he was eighteen," Jean said with a smile, wrapping her arms around her mate.

"Oh. Well, he should be fine."

Wade watched through narrowed eyes, his arms crossed over his chest. His gaze fell on Paige, and his freckles almost seemed to pulse.

Lyle turned to him and nodded once.

Wade turned away, his arms falling to his side.

Doe sighed quietly and put her hand on Paige's arm. "Perhaps you should go lie down. Call it a night."

She probably should. That much power, she should be knocked off her feet and exhausted. How many days would she sleep *this* time? "Yeah."

But she'd lost all her votes.

Leslie needed those votes.

Her unborn children did, too.

And some unknown shifter witch needed them in order to survive.

Paige was going to have to pull something amazing off in the next few days.

TWELVE

PAIGE, for all that she should be tired, couldn't sleep. She slipped out the back and walked along the river's edge until the sun disappeared and the stars came out, letting her mind travel where it wanted. She hadn't had the chance to do that in a really long time and it was therapeutic.

She could hear the occasional skirmishes as paws dug into the dirt. A yip. A growl. She wasn't alone.

Which was fine. She didn't need to be *alone*. She just needed time to herself.

Blessed Mother. She was having twins.

The reality of it kept crashing down around her. She *wasn't* mother of the year. She wasn't even mother of the hour...for an hour. She was the kind of mom the world should be thankful had only spawned once. It wasn't that her daughter was a horrible human being. It was the fact that Paige just wasn't much of a mother. She worked.

Doing whatever the hell *this* was.

Her mind spun back around to the Red Star Division. That needed a solution. And fast. Whatever was going down in Troutdale was bigger than Dexx. The popping of the wards worried Paige more than she wanted to admit. It was a bad sign and she knew it.

But Doe wasn't going to back off.

And her twin babies needed Doe's support.

A thunderbird? Really? And a...a rajasi? How in the world was she pregnant with either of those? She was a *witch*. A witch. And a pretty common one at that.

Okay. Maybe not *super* common, you know, with the ability to pull demons from the hole in her soul—literally— or the fact that she commanded all four elements *and* was capable of touching ley line magick, which was new to her.

But she was a crap witch at spells. And most of all the *other* witch stuff. When it came to craft, Leslie was the better witch.

Leslie.

Fuck. Paige didn't know what to do. Should she be doing anything? *Could* she do anything? What was there to do? Dexx had been okay after he'd been bitten and chosen by a saber-toothed cat. He'd gotten a few lessons from Chuck and everything had turned out pretty okey-dokey.

Except that if Leslie was in Dexx's pack, *Dexx* would be the one teaching her.

Yeah. They were in a world of hurt. Paige loved her man, she did. But if Leslie had to take lessons on how to control a powerful animal spirit from him, they were all screwed. He still couldn't control his shift in the middle of downtown Troutdale, for crying out loud.

Oh boy. And if Leslie was going to have that much trouble, then how hard would it be to raise a thunderbird and a rajasi? And—what did she even know about a rajasi?

Nothing.

She pulled out her phone, coming to a stop, and pulled up Google. It sluggishly answered her. After a few moments, she'd read through everything Google knew on the subject.

Which wasn't a lot.

It was an old Thai myth of a lion with fire for his main, tail, and paws, but it didn't really have information or a point. It was just a lion on fire.

But if he was an ancient and had been—banished? *Had they been banished?*—then there had to be more to it than that.

Paige looked up from her phone and stashed it in her back pocket. She should get back because she wasn't getting anywhere muddling around in her own head.

The river was gone.

The canyon was no longer there.

All that surrounded her was desert.

And the mountain of rocks from the night before.

What the hell was up with this damned desert?

The sand a few yards away shivered then went still.

Paige took a step back, watching it. She called on Cawli's eyes to help her see better, but that didn't help.

The sand quivered again in a long, jagged line that traveled from her feet to the base of the rock where the Spirit Cave had been.

Shit. Paige reached inside herself and touched her magick.

Cawli stared out of her eyes on high alert.

"You don't know what this is, either?" she asked quietly.

I do not.

Great.

The sand shook, harder this time, and pooled, collecting in three spots before rising from the ground and taking form until three women stood in front of her.

Three sand women.

One was young, her dark hair braided on either side of her face. She wore a leather skirt that looked, quite literally, like an animal pelt. She wore no top, but her breasts were bound in leather.

The second was older, taller, and her hair was done up in an intricate bun. Well, it looked fancy. Her hair poofed around her head and ringlets fell artfully around her face. She wore an outfit straight out of the Wild West days. It wasn't a prairie dress. It was more like a fancy traveling dress.

The third was even older. Her long hair was gray and unruly, but she kept it in a long braid down her back. She wore a dress that was even older than the second gal.

"What's this? Christmas past, present, and future?"

The oldest woman stepped forward, holding out her hand. "We are the sand women."

As if that helped explain anything. "Okay. I'm guessing you're here to show me something."

The youngest woman tipped her head to the side. "You are the one who came out here asking questions."

Well, she had. "Can you tell me about the ancients? Or are you going to be as cryptic as everyone else?"

The middle woman glanced at the crone. "I still do not believe this is a good idea."

"Your opinion has been noted." The crone took another step toward Paige. "Paige Whiskey, you have been chosen and you need to know what you're stepping into."

It was about time someone shared this information with her. "What can you tell me?"

The crone gestured with her hand as if telling Paige to take it.

With a sigh, Paige placed her fingertips on the crone's palm.

The nighttime desert setting disappeared and was replaced by green rolling hills, purple flowers, and tall trees for as far as the eye could see. It didn't look like they were in America anymore.

"Where are we?"

The crone glanced up at her. "We are in the old world."

Which meant what? "We're in the past?"

"Yes. Europe, before the coming of the Christians."

Paige blinked. This was starting to feel a little bit like *Outlander*. "Just promise me you won't forget me here."

The crown looked up at her and smiled wryly. "Come. I want to show you."

They walked for a while at a pretty good clip, making Paige's calves burn. She was out of shape. And that probably wasn't a good thing. Eventually, they came across a small town. Small stone buildings with thatched roofs. The streets were muddy from fresh rain, and a wagon was pulling into town.

"What do you see?"

Paige shrugged. She saw people. People walking around, kids playing, people do laundry, pigs, horses, a few cows. The town wasn't big. If she applied herself, she could probably count how many buildings there were. But she wasn't a numbers person, so she just didn't do that naturally. She wagered there were probably less than fifty buildings all total. Though it could be pretty close. "What am I supposed to see?"

The crown pointed. "Look toward the center of town. In what they call the town square."

Paige's human eyes were starting to get old, so she pulled on the power of Cawli and looked with his eyes. There in the center of town was a beast unlike anything she'd seen before. The back-half looked like a lion, but it was winged, and had the head of an eagle. It was a really big eagle. "What is that?"

"That is a griffin."

In all of Paige's research, she didn't think she'd ever actually seen a recollection of a real griffin. She always assumed that they were just pretend creatures like the unicorn and the pegasus. "And unicorns are real too?"

The crone looked at her out of the corner of her eyes. "Of course, they are."

The mammoth hadn't been joking, then. Great. "All right. What am I meant to see?"

The crone snapped her fingers and they were suddenly in the middle of town square.

Paige looked at the old crone. "Why didn't you just do that to begin with?"

The crone smiled and gestured towards the town square.

They stood on the outskirts sheltered by the awning of a shop. People moved around them as if they weren't really there.

She really was the ghost of Christmas past.

After a few moments though, a man in long robes entered the town square and approached the griffin.

The majestic animal picked up his head, his beak opening.

Paige didn't understand birds very well, but she could tell that this particular bird was in pain. He looked exhausted and very tired.

The man raised his right hand palm out. And then an arc of gold light pulled away from the creature and entered the mage's hand, charging it with power.

The griffin cried out as if in pain.

The mage's head fell back and he roared.

The people around them yelled, ducking as if they had been hit with an artillery around. They scrambled, grabbing their loved ones and children and running for safety.

The scene continued to play out like this, the mage taking more and more of the griffin's power.

"What am I supposed to do?" Paige asked quietly.

"The ancients were removed from this world for their safety. They are very powerful creatures, but they have extreme weaknesses."

There had to be a reason the crone was showing her *this* scene, though.

The crone snapped her fingers and the town disappeared. The nighttime desert came back into view, along with the two other women.

Paige stood in the sudden silence. She hadn't realized just how loud the griffin's cries of pain had been. "I don't understand." What did they want her to do? Exactly.

The middle woman stepped forward, a sour expression on her face. She held out her hand.

With a sigh, Paige took it.

The desert setting disappeared again and, this time, Paige stood just outside of her house in Oregon.

Her family was in trouble, being attacked by something Paige couldn't see, but she could sense the immense *power*. Dexx and Leslie fought for their lives.

They were losing.

But then Leslie set her hands on him, and it bolstered him. He got to his feet and glanced down at her. "We're going to make this."

"I hope so." Leslie looked as though she was tiring.

Paige looked to the woman beside her in alarm. This hadn't happened yet. "What's going on? Is this happening right now?"

"No, but it will soon."

"What?" Then, why were they just standing around talking to one another in the desert?

"A very powerful witch is headed your way. He has trapped an ancient and he is going after the others."

"I don't understand. Then why are the ancients coming out now? Cawli said that it was safe."

"Cawli was not wrong, but I fear the reason he got you tangled up in this was so you could free the captured ancient. You can free them all."

The captured ancient? What? Wait. Like the one shifter witch who'd gone crazy and had destroyed Doe's pack. Cawli said the difference was that Leslie had been chosen, her *babes* had been chosen, Doe's shifter witch had been *chosen*. The one who'd killed Doe's pack hadn't been. "How many are captured?"

"Unknown."

"But you just said—"

"You must go to them and reveal yourself."

"What?" They couldn't have been more confusing if they'd strung random words together.

The Whiskey home disappeared and was replaced with desert again, the other two sand women appearing.

"Is this part of the trials?"

"Trials?"

"Yeah, you know. What Doe is doing."

"Those are secondary, child." The old crone smiled, but her eyes flicked to the other two in quick succession. "Doe and her charge will be fine. You must prove yourself worthy to the ancients."

Paige had thought that's exactly what she *had* been doing.

She guessed she'd have to try harder.

THIRTEEN

THE GHOST of Times Past needed to get her story straight. "But you said they're already here, so I think we're a little past that. Don't you?"

"Partially. Your spirit Cawli is the beginning. *Shedim Patesh* has come again."

"Who?"

"Dexx's spirit animal."

"Hattie?"

The crone shook her head, her expression filled with mild disgust. "That is a ridiculous name for a creature so strong."

"Hattie," Paige said with her own derision dripping from her words, "is an incredibly strong name. How many Hattie's have *you* met?" In truth, Paige had only met one, but she'd been one of the most kick-ass ladies she'd ever met. The human Hattie'd known Alma during the war. Paige wasn't sure she was even alive anymore.

The crone shook her head. "She is among the most powerful spirits known, a great deal more powerful than

Cawli. Your sister has been chosen as well. But only *you* can make them come."

"That doesn't make sense. Leslie's already been chosen. These kids I'm carrying have too and I'm still 'the only one who can make them come?' You're talking in circles."

"If you fail here, the griffin will not come forward and your babies will not... make it."

"They won't... make it?" As in be born? Was that seriously what she was saying?

The crone was quiet for a long moment. "Yes."

Paige didn't even know what to say to that. The heaviness in her chest felt like a brick.

"They need the power you possess. You are what your 'packs' need to rebalance themselves."

"So, Leslie doesn't need Doe?"

The crone shrugged dismissively. "It will not hurt to stay together, but they need you whole and complete."

"By whole and complete, you mean..."

The one who hadn't spoken yet held out a hand. "Fully yourself, in full mastery of your abilities."

"All of them," the crone said.

Cawli really should have warned her about this. "So, what I'm seeing here is a catch twenty-two. If I fail in bringing the ancients, my babies die. If I succeed in bringing them, people might die because they're so powerful. Did I leave anything out?"

The crone gestured that she was correct.

"Why would I even volunteer for this?" Because Paige was frustrated with people telling her what she should do for others. "Why would I endanger my family? My kids? What's in it for me?"

The crone sighed. "They do..." She licked her lips.

"They add flavor to the world that has been missing for a very long time. There are others who will flourish with the ancients. Dryads and the fairy folk, for instance, will be stronger for having them in our world."

"And us? What about my family?"

"If you survive this, you will be a force to be reckoned with."

"Don't ask for a hell of a lot, do you? And how am I supposed to prove my worthiness?" Paige was full to bursting with the things she *had* to be. *Had* to do.

"Go to them. Present yourself and be judged."

"I've already gone to the Spirit Cave."

The crone said nothing.

Something in Paige snapped. "Well, how the *fuck* do I do that? Google it? Ask for directions? Or should I pray to them like the angels are so fond of asking."

"You have a guide already. A word of warning though. You must not hold back. They are the ancients."

"Hold what back? My powers? Should I go there, wherever it is, and start blasting everything I find? You have to give me more than that."

"Go to them and present yourself. We know nothing more than that." The old crone pushed Paige backward.

The scene dispersed into the spirit cave again.

A big, white tiger stood next to the pure blue waters. He glowed with a familiar pull.

Cawli.

"You knew?" She said it out loud, but no echoes came back.

You do not understand, he said, his voice sounding constrained, *the effort it took to create a line of witches capable of supporting the most powerful of our ancients.*

"What does that mean?"

He whuffed. *Do you recall your bloodline?*

Of course she did. It interfolded so many times, it made her hear banjo music in the back of her head.

There is a reason so much effort went into your birth.

"These ancients. Why now? And don't tell me because it's safe for them to come here. Why send them out here to be possibly hunted if you don't have to?"

Cawli didn't say anything for a long time. *They are being hunted in our world.*

She sensed it was a bit more than that. "You can hunt them down, track them down. Why not do that?"

Someone from your world—a shifter witch not of our choosing—has captured the oldest of us, the great stag.

"So," she said, struggling to put the pieces together, "you chose us so you could hunt the person who trapped your deer."

That is crudely put, but yes.

Paige snarled. "Then why do *I* have to *present* myself to this group of ancient spirits? This is stupid. To see how I'd enjoy being used?"

When you give birth, do you not choose someone worthy to bring the child out? So, too, we choose someone worthy to bring us forth.

That didn't even make sense. She'd go see a doctor to ensure she didn't *die* while giving birth. Paige crushed her teeth together. "Fine. Let's get presented."

Come to me.

She had no idea what that was going to do, but she closed the distance between them. Reaching out to touch him, she dug her fingers into his soft, thick fur. He felt amazing.

Witch. There were many voices in that word, but Paige had no idea where the word had come from.

Cawli turned and stood in front of Paige. He was enormous. His shoulders weren't as tall as Hattie's but he seemed well-matched to her. Like they were part of the same being.

What in the hell was she up against?

Cawli dipped his head to Paige and touched her forehead. It was much the same as Chuck had done before he put her on the plane.

You must go. Show yourself to them and don't hold anything back.

"I've already done this."

Not like this.

Damnit. Why couldn't anyone just be plain with what they wanted her to do?

Paige stepped around Cawli, dragging her fingers against his fur. It was soft and warm, just like Dexx when he shifted.

Above the water, a mist formed in the dark. It swirled and broke apart into glowing, distinct patches.

The light split, then split again, and kept splitting until the lake was lit by spirits. Blues, golds, reds, and greens populated the air above the lake.

Holy shit. There was a lot of them.

Paige stopped at the water's edge. She held up a hand. "Hello?"

Witch, hundreds of voices said again.

She was tired of hearing that. "Yes. We all know I'm a witch. Please stop telling me what I know."

"You have spirit. When confronted with superior power, not many take the offensive," a single deep and calming voice said.

Was it the glowing dot in the middle? "Well, the only instruction I got was not to hold back. So, you get it all."

Thank you. That voice warmed her soul. It was deep, red, and comforting.

Another voice interrupted, this one higher pitched. *She has been marked by a door inside her.*

The Hell gate. Was she supposed to say something to that?

It leads to a great power like the Great War. I don't think we should get involved.

The Great War, huh? With that statement came a small inrush of images, of the ancients fighting angels and demons in their true forms.

That couldn't be possible. Could it?

This child has more power that she should. Great power. She is the nexus.

A nexus? To what? "How about talking to me?" Paige let her frustration out. "I know I'm only a silly little human, but you wanted to talk. And I have—" She waved her hand around. "—all that power. Maybe I could be part of the discussion?"

Cawli turned his massive feline head toward her and it almost looked like he smiled.

The mass of lights hovering over the lake flickered randomly.

Paige sat down on a rock, waiting.

The lights began to move in slight circles. They swirled and danced, and somewhere in the chaos, they arranged themselves in tiers.

The lowest levels had most of the glowing orbs. The highest held only one light, golden and swollen larger than the rest.

The lowest level of lights faded out.

What was going on?

The next tier of light disappeared.

"Did I say something wrong?" She had lost all of her votes with the alphas. If this went poorly too, she was sunk. Dexx. Leslie. Her kids. Her heart leapt in her throat.

These...ancients?

The tiers of the lights faded until there were seven left. The great golden orb shot soft shafts of light into the cavern ceiling.

Every one of the seven blue lights changed. They formed into glowing heads of mythical animals.

The two on either end were her unborn twins.

The bird head in the middle spoke. *You are a witch. There are reasons we have chosen to stay away. There are reasons we should continue to do so. However, our time is needed. Something great and vast is rising and you will need us.*

That sounded ominous. "What's coming?"

The two heads on either side of the bird head tinged with red. *If the signs are right, then* she *will be chosen by another.*

The light above them blinked blue then pink then blue again.

And the one who chooses her was removed to protect us all.

Some believe so, the spirit at the top said.

That left it open to interpretation. But she who was going to be chosen by another? What did that even mean?

I am coming. The bird head was large and looked like an eagle, maybe. Not that Paige knew her birds really well. He had tufts where his ears might be if he was a mammal. "Prepare the Great Cat. I come. She has led us before and I accept her lead again."

We are coming, her children said in unison. *The way will be hard. Prepare yourself.*

"What did that mean, prepare the great cat?" Did he mean Dexx? How could she prepare Dexx for this? She didn't even have a handle on what she saw, let alone tell anyone else about it so they could...*prepare.*

Be ready, the voices said in unison. *You are the battle leader. There are no innocents in war. And this is war.*

The cave faded and the stars came back.

Cawli settled back fully in her mind. Something was different. She felt... squirmy. Not the kind that led to the inability to sit still, but the kind that made her insides feel not completely stable.

Purely against her will, Paige's eyes slid closed. No, she couldn't sleep. There was too much to be explained. What was coming? Why did they need the ancients? Exactly *what* were the ancients? The griffin had said ...

Paige sat up suddenly. The first shafts of bright sunlight stabbed at her eyes. The rocky desert still surrounded her, but the cold night air was held back by coyotes?

Six of them curled against her. They slowly rose to their paws.

Paige wasn't certain what was going on, but she was glad she hadn't frozen out there on her own. She had heard the desert got quite cold at night. "Coffee."

One of the coyotes shifted into Erica, her wild, red hair cascading down her back. "We were sent to keep you alive. Don't think this means we like you. Or trust you."

"Coffee." Paige hadn't realized she'd gone to sleep in the first place, but now that it was morning, her personality needed caffeine.

Erica tipped her head to the side. "You've seen shifters before?"

"What, naked? Of course, I have. Dexx's pack is around all the time. I see more asses than a proctologist. It's fine."

The woman grinned and stood. "Then, we need to get back. Your trials aren't done, and the sooner we can be rid of you, the better."

FOURTEEN

PAIGE WENT BACK to Doe's and slept until the following morning.

Probably wasn't the best thing she could have done, but at least it wasn't days this time. When she got up, she was greeted with the aroma of fresh brewed coffee and bacon.

The midget ancients growing inside her womb did worm-sized acrobatics.

It was odd that she could "feel" them when she knew they were so small. Well, they might be bigger. What did she know? She'd been pregnant once before, but that had been fourteen years ago.

Shit. What was she thinking having another baby? Now?

Doe turned around at the stove and looked at Paige for a long moment before turning back to the stove. "Are you feeling better?"

"I am." Paige could feel the migraine coming. She hadn't had caffeine in almost an entire day. If she didn't get some in her system now, she was going to have a migraine for the rest of the day. "What's on the schedule for today?"

Doe sighed. "Nothing."

Dread settled in the pit of Paige's gut. "What?"

"You lost all of your votes and now there's no real point."

No real point. "I disagree."

"Feel free to, but the reality is that you lost."

She really hadn't. Paige leaned against the counter. "I guess I lost when it came to your pack, but I gained the information I needed, information that might help you with *your* shifter witch. Which, by the way, is she still alive?"

Doe twitched. "He is."

"Oh, good. Because he's needed, I guess, for some big bad thing that's coming? There's a reason the ancients are showing up. And it's more than the fact they need a bounty hunter or something to track down the person who trapped their leader."

Doe raised an eyebrow.

Paige waved her off. "Yeah. I know. And it's more than the fact that ancients want to come out and play or that it's 'safe' for them to do so."

"It is not."

"I agree. But..." Paige had a lot of information to wrap her head around. "There's something big coming and they're offering their help to stop it."

"Big like your angels and demons?"

Paige accepted the cup of coffee Doe offered her. "I think? I don't know. Maybe."

Doe set her spatula down. "Our seer sees a big change on the horizon. Many, in fact. It has me spooked."

"I think Chuck is too. That's maybe why he's doing everything he can to gather as many power players to him as he can."

"It is a good idea." Doe's tone said that even though

Paige hadn't completed her trials or passed them that she wasn't entirely sure abandoning Chuck was a wise choice. "I had to hoped to discover if you were what brought the destruction."

That was a horrible thought. "I hope no—" But what if she was?

Doe blinked and met her gaze, waiting.

But maybe not in the same way they originally thought. "Maybe I don't personally blow things up. Maybe, just maybe, I am responsible because I haven't brought Sven to justice."

"The angel?"

"No, the, uh, demon who was *with* the angel. Okay. You know what? Those two are powerful trouble and they're bigger than I am on my own. So, okay? Just don't judge."

Doe nodded, her jaw canted. "What ancients are you bringing?"

Paige groaned internally. "A griffin chose my sister and I'm carrying a thunderbird and a rajasi."

Doe closed her eyes for a long moment. "Why so many? I didn't think you were looking to gain more power in your witch family."

"We're not." Paige cringed, wondering just how Doe was going to take this. "It looks like we're going to be the center of this war, though."

"Your children?"

Paige didn't even want to think about that. "If my children are to be a part of this war, then, we at least have time to prepare."

"At least there's that."

If there was something on the horizon, it gave them time to heal whatever rift stood between their peoples as well. "We're so screwed, Doe. I don't even know what to do."

Doe turned off the burner and leaned against the counter beside Paige. "You were chosen."

That wasn't helping.

"Not once, but three times."

"My kids were chosen. They're going to be people, you know. They're not mini-me's."

Doe gave Paige a frank look. "But the only way for them to choose your children is to meet and chose you first. They must think you and your mate are quite worthy."

"I doubt it. We're just like normal people. We fuck up just like everyone else." Which was the truest statement ever.

Doe opened her mouth to say something, but was interrupted.

Mahir burst through the back door. "Doe, he's gone."

"What do you mean gone?"

He glanced at Paige, and then dismissed her. "Exactly what I said."

Doe pushed off the counter, ignoring the food. "Signs? Smells?"

Mahir shook his head and turned back to the door, leading the way out.

Paige didn't know what she was *supposed* to do, but she wasn't the type of person who just sat idly by doing nothing when something went wrong. She decided to keep her mouth shut though. She hadn't actually been invited in.

"He's just gone. Without a trace."

Doe led them out the door. "I find that hard to believe."

Paige followed them around the side of the house where they had a shed. The lock was gone, the chain dangling on the handle. "What—" She probably should just stay out of this, but... "What did you have in here?"

Doe glanced at her, clearly not wanting to have this conversation. "A child."

"This is what you did to your shifter witch?"

"We were trying to hide him." Doe sighed resigned. "But... we failed, obviously."

"Hide?" Paige poked her head inside the shed and found it had been converted into a comfortable bedroom. At least there was that. "What spirit chose him?"

"Pegasus." Doe turned back to the shed. "He was a boy from a local witch family. A troupe of vampires came through town and wiped them out."

Vampires? Was this about to get weird? "What?"

"We don't have a problem with witches, not like in Oregon. We actually have—*had*—a good relationship with them, but then one of our kids bit their boy. None of us thought anything of it."

Sounded like what happened with Leslie. "And then months later, he started changing?"

Doe shook her head. "I could feel the power rising almost instantly."

"Like Chuck."

"Yeah. We've been trying to keep him safe, but others can feel this power, too."

Did that mean that others could sense Leslie's power? The twins' power? Were they drawing packs of vampires to their town? Well, probably not vampires. They went blood crazed just stepping into the area, but rogue packs? "You kept him in a shed."

"Only until you left. We were hoping you could...help." The look on Doe's face told Paige exactly what she thought of her "help."

Oh, enough with the kid gloves. Paige rolled her head, popping her neck. "Just stay out of my way."

Cawli's voice came out a little, dark and growly.

Using his senses, she sniffed the air.

"I doubt you can find him. We're better at this than you."

"How would you know?" Paige and Cawli asked, her tone different when laced with her cat. "You haven't met us."

The air was blank of scents, even fine ones.

Completely blank.

Masking?

Paige tipped her head to the side and listened.

Crickets scurried in the dirt.

The blades of grass whispered together as they danced on the wind.

The daisies beat a brief staccato on the side of the shed.

A heartbeat raced, small and erratic.

Rabbit, Cawli told her.

She wasn't finding anything using her spirit senses. She reached deep inside of herself and pulled on her connections to the All Mother.

Earth answered quickly, eager to find one of her children. The thought thread raced along the roots of the grass, the trees, and the wildflowers, seeking.

Wind danced around Paige's head, tugging at her hair, ready to be released, to search and play and seek and find. With the target in mind, it scurried away, chattering excitedly to itself, a small ball of energy.

Water trickled up through the roots and burbled at Paige's feet. It grabbed onto the call and latched onto it.

Fire rumbled below the earth's surface, eager for release.

Not that day. Paige thanked it, but let it go.

Reluctantly, it followed her request.

The earth shot back a pinging signal, almost like radar.

The water quivered and sent a signal as if with sonar.

The air squealed in excitement and screamed like a tiny tornado around Paige's head, pulling her hair from her braid and running away in the direction of the river.

Paige didn't wait. She ran, following the air and the water and the earth, doing their bidding and following their signal.

She heard someone call out to her, but she was too connected, too close. She was going to find this boy and keep him safe. Safe from the shifters and the witches and the people wanting to control him.

She ran, power in her legs pushing her faster than she'd ever gone before. The orchard trees whooshed by, leaves and petals raining down behind her. Her legs propelled her to the river, and then along the river bottom. She leapt onto a large boulder, and then off the other side. Her mind was ultra-focused. Cawli helped her focus her leg's power to gain the most ground with the least amount of wasted effort.

Use caution, Cawli said.

A whiff of something coppery and tainted tingled her nostrils. She stopped and hid behind a copse of trees, scanning the immediate area.

Three wolves and four coyotes slid in behind her.

The timber wolf morphed into Doe, tall and naked. She crouched down beside Paige, giving her a furtive glance as she did. "Why did you stop?"

"A scent." Paige blinked, feeling a little more...human. That was the thing with the elements. When they spoke loudly, she didn't *feel* her emotions, not like a human did, anyway. Not like a mortal. She pointed just ahead. "The air and the water both agree that the boy is just there."

"The air and the water?" Lyle said, his hair no longer

pulled up in a man-bun and cascading down his wide shoulders.

Paige nodded, trying to get a better location. Air and water weren't the best for that. They could tell her general locations, but earth... "I'm waiting for earth to give me an exact location."

Doe glanced at Lyle, and then at the other shifters.

Erica had shifted, her red hair wild around her. "What do we do? What's the plan?"

Paige turned to her. "The plan is easy. I go in. I get the boy. I get out."

Wade morphed, talking before his fur shifted to freckles. "And how are you going to do that? Do you have any idea what you're up against? What numbers?"

"I will." The earth rumbled at her fingertips. Paige dug her fingers into the rocky soul of the riverbank and closed her eyes. The earth tugged her along the root system, passed the river on the other side, through a spread of grass roots and to the base of a very large tree.

The tree itself hummed, young and big and fresh. Rushing up the trunk, following the curves of life force, Paige saw through the eyes of the tree, through the leaves. At first, it was hard to make out, but as she pieced the images together, she understood.

"They look human. There's twelve of them."

"Twelve." Doe's tone wasn't happy.

Paige focused on what else the tree could tell her.

The only thing it said was, *Dead.*

"Vampires?" she asked.

The tree didn't have an answer.

"That's what attacked his people before."

Paige didn't know how to fight vampires.

I do, Cawli rumbled quietly.

Oh, good. But first, there was something Paige had to clear up. She blinked, releasing the call of the elements. Earth sighed and slipped back.

Paige turned to Doe. "Is this a trial." It wasn't a question. She made it a statement because she was almost certain she knew the answer. Everything was too coincidental. It had to be a test, in which case, she had to be very careful not to *kill* anyone.

Doe's eyes flashed. "No."

It seemed like she was telling the truth. Paige looked out across the river. "Do you think they kidnapped him for his own good?"

"They killed his family who were our allies and under our protection," Doe said. "So, no."

"You weren't exaggerating or telling a story."

"No."

That was all Paige needed to know. "I'm going to kill them."

"You will need our help."

Probably not. Paige was still in the high of elemental-talk and Cawli's pushing at her to hunt and to kill wasn't helping. "Then follow and try not to die."

"How about," Wade said with no small amount of derision, "you try not to get in our way."

Paige smiled slightly, gathering power in her legs. She sprang, leaping over the river and landing gracefully on the opposite bank.

She'd *never* been that graceful before.

The wolves and the coyotes followed with equal grace.

She didn't wait for them. Paige ran toward the tree. She could feel it like a homing beacon in her heart. Once she got there, she didn't wait. She attacked.

Two men turned toward her, their fangs out, their fingers curled with claws. They looked sickly and pale.

Paige swung her hand and caught one across the throat with her claws. She slammed the other one with a powerful gale.

A third vampire rushed Paige.

She hit it with her witch hands, blowing its shadow from the body which fell to the ground like a sack of potatoes.

Was that its soul she'd blasted away?

She didn't have time to think about it.

She called earth and air, mixed it with just enough fire, and reached out with her hand, feeling a little like Thor waiting for his hammer. She clenched her fist then yanked it downward.

Lightning split the air and another vampire exploded into a fine mist drifting to the desert floor.

She'd never been able to create lightning before and she was afraid to think about the ramifications of that in that moment.

The vampire she hit with the wind started to rise. Doe in her wolf form and another wolf pounced on the vampire and ravaged it. They spared no quarter and tore it to pieces.

The boy cowered from two women vampires. His hands and feet were bound with a rough rope.

Paige moved in his direction as two more vampires rose.

Between one instant and another, the entire landscape changed. The disappeared into desert. Big rock outcroppings hid several of her opponents from view as a canyon jutted up from the ground.

But this wasn't a vision like before when the spirits had spoken to her, and this wasn't a real shifting of the earth because the element was quiet in her hands.

This was an illusion.

One of the vampires jumped and grappled her to the ground, lunging for her with its teeth.

With her arms pinned she brought earth forward. It rumbled through the ground in sharp spears, angry and eager to be used.

The vampire dodged most of the sharp stone jabbing forward but still took a lance to the arm. She screamed but kept up the fight for Paige's throat.

Vampires were disgusting creatures when they were in full bloodlust.

Paige scrambled from beneath the biting vampire and called fire. It wasn't the gentle fire most witches called. This was the earth's fire, lava. It seeped out of the ground, inching toward the vampires, lighting them on fire with a touch.

Doe and her pack had killed another two vampires and were facing off with another.

This one had skill. He managed to keep the wolves in front of him and from flanking him. He moved forward like a snake, snapping a fist into a wolf's side, sending it sprawling,

"Enough." Paige stood still and calm calling all the elements together. The only way to keep everyone safe was to end this quickly and with the elements so close to her, she understood the most efficient way to deal with this issue.

Her witch hands swung out and battered the three remaining vampires. The earth sprang up as a wall of lava behind the vampires.

The air solidified and trapped them against the stone and water rose up from cracks in the ground.

The tree's limbs snapped out and grabbed the survivors,

wrapping them up in wood and leaves until all that was visible was enlarged tree branches.

The wolves and coyotes jogged back, and they shifted back to humans.

Paige came to her senses to quiet. She turned to Doe, a little winded. As the elements left her, her humanity rushed back in with an emotional weight like led. She'd never been *that* deep inside the elements before and she didn't think she wanted to do that again any time soon. "Are we hurt?"

Doe stood as a naked woman and raised a single eyebrow, ignoring her question. "You have your votes. You can tell Chuck we will see him when he asks."

FIFTEEN

PAIGE FINISHED PACKING her things into her suitcase and zipped it up.

Doe leaned against the doorframe. "What are you going to do now?"

Paige had no frelling clue. "Go home. Make sure Dexx didn't burn the house down." She could almost hear him say, *I didn't burn the house down* in that tone he always used. "And then protect my sister when she needs me."

"And what about..." Doe gestured toward Paige's abdomen.

"Well, I'm going to try not dying and not killing them." First and foremost.

Doe chuckled. "That would probably be a good idea."

"Yeah." Paige sighed and thumped her suitcase with one hand. "I don't know. I'm a little worried. How many more ancients are coming and what does it mean? What is this big bad and how best do we prepare for it?"

Doe shook her head. "We're going to keep a watch out for more, but right now, it's only him and you."

"Keep him safe."

"I thought for sure you would want to take him back with you."

"As interesting as that sounds, no." Paige meant it, too. "We have enough going on as it is. I don't know how 'powerful' a pegasus is, but Cawli cautioned me about how powerful *all* the ancients are."

"Do you think he's one?"

"Who?"

"Cawli."

That was something Paige hadn't even considered. "I don't know, but I don't think so."

Doe nodded. "Okay. You be safe."

"I will certainly try. You keep that boy out of trouble. Find someone to teach him his witch ways. There are many good people out there who can."

"We will."

"And if you need help with him..."

"I'll call."

Paige smiled and grabbed her bag.

Doe didn't move out of the way.

Licking her lips, Paige scuffed her toe. "Is there something else you wanted to say?"

"Well..." Doe shook her head once. "You were really powerful back there, when we were saving Max."

Yeah. A lot more powerful than she'd felt in a long time.

"It was a little scary."

Paige didn't know what she should say to that.

"Do you think—"

Paige waited.

Doe shook her head again and raised her chin. "Just make sure you don't give witches a bad name."

"I haven't yet."

Doe smiled and stepped back, giving Paige the right of way. "I'll let Chuck know he's got an invitation."

Doe nodded. "Have a good flight."

Yeah. Paige planned on it.

But first, she had to save Dexx and his team from murder charges, and then find a better way to keep her children safe.

From her unborn children.

Dexx Colt, demon hunter extraordinaire, yanked the wheel hard to the right and stabbed the gas pedal.

Jackie, his '70 Dodge Challenger, responded, throwing him back in the seat. Her rear end swung sideways. Smoke rolled off the new rubber, and Jackie jetted forward.

The red Mini Cooper they pursued held its own. That really shouldn't be possible, but Dexx had fallen behind on maintaining Jackie with everything else going on.

"Come on, girl." They blew past a stop sign and turned onto Main. "You don't want to get shown up by a Mini Coupe, do you?"

Rainbow Blu gripped the door handle, releasing a sharp yelp.

Dexx opened up Jackie's stroked 440. The torque pushed them hard into the seats as she climbed towards redline. Pavement shook as she roared down the street. It was noon, so Main was busy.

One guy opened his car door, only to close it and suck in close to his parked car. A woman dragged her teenaged son who was paying more attention to his phone than where he was walking back to the median. A group of college-aged women held their phones up, but whether it was to take selfies or to capture the chase, Dexx wasn't sure.

He also didn't have time to care.

Being a detective meant high-speed car chases. Jackie had been born for this. They loved it when the bad guys ran.

Except when they ran on foot.

The little red car swerved across the lanes, keeping Dexx and Rainbow behind him. The Mini Cooper clipped a car stopped at the light with his rear end, knocking the mirror off and shattering the driver's side window.

Dexx avoided hitting things with Jackie for obvious reasons. He respected the hell out of her, for one.

Several sharp corners let the little sportster gain ground. It darted in between traffic, cutting people off. A chorus of honks followed them. Oncoming traffic stopped, which wasn't helping. He still preferred that, rather than trying to guess how they might dodge. The average person wasn't great at defensive driving.

Chief Tuck would be pissed. Again.

"What'd you say this guy's name was?" Dexx asked conversationally.

Rainbow took in a sharp breath. She clamped her eyes closed, her afro bobbing with Jackie's movements. "Jeremy. Jeremy Stevens."

Average sounding name.

Rainbow let out a screech as they drift-turned onto another street. They narrowly missed a pedestrian who—for some reason—thought it was safe to enter the crosswalk behind the speeding Mini Cooper. "We're going to die."

"Negative, sweetheart. Not today." At least, not while *he* had the wheel.

"I know it. We're dead."

Was she hyperventilating? This damned chase had been her idea. "Get Tuck on the line. We need a little help here."

Rainbow nodded, but her hands didn't move. One gripped the seat, the other the door handle.

Dexx pulled his phone off the seat beside him and slammed it on her lap. "Call!"

Rainbow let go of the seat and grabbed the phone. She looked sick. "Dexx..."

"No," Dexx bellowed. "You puke in here, you really *will* die. Man up, woman!"

The Mini Cooper ran a red light, his little engine screaming as he shot past Main again. The car zoomed through the intersection tearing the rear bumper from an old tan rust bucket truck spinning it into oncoming traffic. Another car slammed into it.

Dexx mashed the gas, narrowly missing the wreck.

"We better end this soon or someone is going to get hurt." Or worse, Jackie will. The world would end if Jackie was wrecked.

"What?" It looked like Rainbow might finally be close to doing something on the phone.

"Just call."

Rainbow wasn't a good cop. Or much of anything else. Paige—his girlfriend or mate or wife or whatever they were—had a soft spot for her, but mostly she just made Paige happy. But Captain Paige Whiskey had the right to hire and fire whoever she damned well pleased, thank you very much.

The little sportster turned a hard left into an alley.

Dexx followed bare seconds later. The alley between the two buildings was narrow enough to block with a flick of the wheel.

He didn't need to.

The red car stopped a few feet away. Jeremy got out, glancing at Dexx. With a grin, he spun and ran.

"Shit." The fucker was running. "Call for backup!"

Not fun. Not even a little. And the day had started out so promising. Sunshine and a little light stakeout. What more could a man ask for?

Jeremy ran to the tall fence at the end of the alley.

If Dexx was chasing a human, he might think this would end soon, but Dexx only dealt with paranormals. So...

He sighed as he got out and watched Jeremy leap over the fence like it was nothing.

Great, but there was a reason Dexx chased paranormals. He was one, too. *You ready for this, Hattie?*

Hattie, the spirit of the saber-toothed cat that had bonded with him, didn't respond. Instead, power pooled in his chest and legs, giving him the power to leap over the fence as effortlessly as Jeremy.

"Dexx, wait," Rainbow Blu called from behind. She sounded like she was shouting through a tunnel.

Dexx's shirt and pants tightened.

Ah, crap! Now wasn't the time for a shift. He'd needed a boost in power, not to turn into a damned extinct cat in broad daylight.

His prey jumped up to a fire escape, leaping from landing to landing up the building.

Why did they always go up?

Dexx's pants shredded. He needed to get this under control, but once Hattie started coming out, there was nothing to stop her.

His clothes fell away. His human limbs morphed into the largest damned cat in the animal kingdom.

The largest damned cat to leap up a fire escape built for humans, not car-sized animals.

The metal groaned with each pounce until it crumpled with a tortured screech.

Well, it hadn't come completely off the building. It was still useable.

Mostly.

His prey was on the roof. At least there, Dexx and his big-assed cat body would have room to maneuver.

Jeremy took off in giant strides, leaping farther than any mundane could.

Now, see that had been what Dexx had wanted to achieve. Power to his *human* legs while *saving* his only set of clothes.

Dexx gathered power in his haunches, relishing in his cat body. Hattie was a natural hunter. Chasing prey was amazing. The smells of the town heightened. His vision narrowed to a pinpoint. He could only see the running man.

Dexx launched himself over a large, roof-mounted fan and tackled the man into the gravel-lined roof, his giant paws pressed into the man's back.

Through Hattie's eyes, the man's head emitted a dark, blue smoke. Hattie growled low, and a dark feeling of unease overwhelmed Dexx. Something was wrong with this man. He needed to end, to cease existence. Hattie opened her mouth and settled her long fangs against the prey's smoky, pulsating throat.

"No," Jeremy panted, "please don't."

Dexx growled, whether at the perp or himself for letting Hattie take control—again—or at Hattie for pushing him out of the way in his own damned body, was a tossup. *Hattie, shift back. Now.*

Hattie closed their jaws.

Hattie, stop!

What set her off? Did it have to do with the blue smoke? Was she seeing something he wasn't?

Whatever it was, Hattie wanted this man dead.

Primordial rage oozed like a sickness into his chest. *You must kill it.* Hattie's deep, rich voice filled his mind.

I ate breakfast already. It was a real trick to get Hattie to cool down after she got this riled, though, honestly, he'd never *seen* her *this* upset. *I need to question him. While he's alive.*

You must kill it. Her voice deepened. *It must be eradicated. It feels wrong. It's too old.*

That's a man, and all the information we have says he's a shifter. Dexx pushed with his mind, willing his hands to replace paws, his human legs to replace the powerful cat haunches.

He's not a shifter.

What the hell was going on with her? Rainbow might not be a great cop, but she was excellent at gathering information. He doubted she'd get this wrong. He needed to regain control and get his body back.

Hattie's will was formidable. Her haunches tensed.

His thighs relaxed.

Her claws extended.

His fingers clenched.

Her jaw tightened.

His jaw loosened, giving Jeremy a chance to breathe.

This was a shifter matter but still fell under human jurisdiction. Jeremy hadn't broken a paranormal law. If Dexx killed him in the human world, even as a newly formed shifter, he would still face severe consequences.

His life was just now starting to shape up into something... decent. He wasn't going to give that up just because his fat fucking cat got a wild hair up her damned ass.

Slowly, Dexx shifted back to a human, one inch at a time.

Until he was nothing more than a naked human man on a roof in the middle of town.

He pressed Jeremy's head down with one hand, grabbing his wrist and pressing it into his back. Dexx felt like a perv. "You owe me new clothes, asshole."

Paige was going to kill him.

Rainbow arrived a minute later with a bundle of shredded fabric.

"Um, Dexx, what's this?" She pulled a bright red rag out of the pile.

Those were a pair of red, silk underwear, which Rainbow knew. He could tell by the snarky tone of her voice. Some people wore mismatched socks. Dexx loved the touch of silk on his butt cheeks. "I got dressed in the dark. Don't tell Paige. Please." Because that particular pair was hers.

Rainbow held her smirk for almost two seconds. "Sure. Your secret's safe with me. Tiger."

"Cat. Just get over here and hold him."

Jeremy struggled a little as Rainbow dropped the clothes and took over for Dexx completely at ease with his nakedness.

Another sign that he was the only one who had a problem with him being naked.

"Sorry, Jeremy. I have to do this."

Every single time she cuffed someone, she apologized. Another reason Dexx didn't think she deserved to be on the team.

Rainbow clicked the cuffs in place. "Spelled cobalt. You won't be able to shift."

Something about that statement made Dexx feel uneasy. Hattie had said he wasn't a shifter and if anyone would know, she would. "You're sure he's a shifter."

Rainbow just shrugged.

Dexx hadn't asked any questions when he'd agreed to help her, but he worried now. "Did you make the call?" he asked, wrapping his shirt around his waist to cover the most important parts.

"Well, I..." She shrugged, gesturing to Jeremy, her mouth open for a moment. "You took off so fast, and I had to catch up, and then—"

"You didn't call." Something was off, even for her. "You know it's not that warm out today, right?"

"I know." She glanced significantly down. "I saw."

"Forget what you saw," Dexx growled.

Shifters who were born to this walked around without

clothes like it didn't matter, which was something Dexx was still trying to get used to. For him, it was still an issue, especially since they were in the middle of town. How was he getting back to his car without any clothes? Chief Tuck might understand about the paranormal, but he still had to enforce human laws like indecent exposure.

"Okay, tough guy." Dexx pulled Jeremy to his feet. "You want to tell me what you're doing for the Eastwood's, and we'll get along much easier."

The Eastwoods were a coven of witches that he and the Whiskey witches had taken down months ago. They'd managed to throw the Eastwood leader in jail, but the coven hadn't dissolved. It was just under new leadership. They were blood magick witches. Dexx was pretty certain they were going to fall back to their old ways at some point.

So, he'd had Rainbow keep an eye on them.

She'd brought him Jeremy as a possible lead.

Jeremy raised an eyebrow at Rainbow with a slight smirk.

What was that all about?

He turned that smirk to Dexx and tipped his head.

"Ah." Dexx grimaced, really wishing for pants. He *was* a damned sexy beast, but even he preferred to intimidate men with his pants *on*. "That's how you're going to play it?"

Dexx probably should have asked a few more questions.

Truth be told, he'd been going a little nuts lately. He might be settling into a good life, but that life involved kids and BBQ's. The kinds of things he wasn't familiar with. He was a demon hunter, not a soccer mom.

Jeremy ducked his head with a shrug. "Look, man. I deal in vending machines. Candy and snacks. That's not a crime."

"It is if you're vending blood or shifters." There were

reports on Dexx's desk about missing shifters in the Portland-Troutdale area. He wasn't sure that Jeremy had anything to do with those, but he needed information. Those reports had been piling up on his desk for weeks with zero leads. "Where's your vending truck, asshole?"

Rainbow moved away, her gaze flitting from Dexx to Jeremy.

She smelled nervous. Why? He was growing suspicious. Did Jeremy even *have* anything to do with the Eastwoods?

It was time to get answers, the real kind.

Dexx grabbed a handcuffed wrist and started walking.

Jeremy turned his attention to Rainbow as they marched to the stairs. He mumbled something, too low for even Dexx to hear.

"Got something you want to say?" Dexx stopped.

Jeremy remained silent.

"Thought so." Something fishy was going on here.

Rainbow stood there staring at Jeremy like a doe in headlights.

"Hey!" Dexx said sharply.

Rainbow jerked her eyes up.

"It's still cold out here."

Join us in *Big, Bad Djinn* as Dexx leads Red Star to deal with the return of Mike Jones, a villainous angel bent on revenge and angelic salvation.

https://www.fjblooding.com/big-bad-djinn

S.S. WOLFRAM
F.J. BLOODING
WHISKEY WITCHES
ANCIENTS
BOOK 2
BIG BAD
DJINN

ALSO BY F.J. BLOODING

Whiskey Witches Universe

Whiskey Witches

Whiskey Witches

Blood Moon Magick

Barrel of Whiskey

Witches of the West

Whiskey Witches: Ancients

Desert Shaman

Big Bad Djinn

Lizard Wizard

Whiskey on the Rocks

Double-Double Demon Trouble

Mirror, Mirror Demon Rubble

Dead Demon Die

Whiskey Witches: Para Wars

Whiskey Storm

London Bridge Down

Midnight Whiskey

International Team of Mystery

Slipping on Karma Peels

Pre-order now at: https://www.fjblooding.com/preorder

Other Books in the Whiskey-Verse

Shifting Heart Romances

by Hattie Hunt & F.J. Blooding

Bear Moon

Grizzly Attraction

Here's the reading order to make it even easier to catch up!

https://www.fjblooding.com/reading-order

Other Books by F.J. Blooding

Devices of War Trilogy

Fall of Sky City

Sky Games

Whispers of the Skyborne

Discover more, sign up for updates and gifts, and join the forum discussions at www.fjblooding.com.

WHISKEY MAGICK & MENTAL HEALTH

SIGN UP TO learn more about our books and receive this free e-zine about Whiskey Magick and Mental Health. https://www.fjblooding.com/books-lp

ABOUT THE AUTHOR

F.J. Blooding lives in hard-as-nails Alaska growing grey hair in the midnight sun with Shane, her writing partner and husband, his two part-time kids, his BrotherTwin, SistaWitch, TeenMan, and SnarkGirl, along with a small menagerie of animals which includes several cats, an army of chickens, a rabbit or two, but only one dog.

She enjoys writing and creating with her wonderful husband and dreaming about sleeping. She's dated vampires, werewolves, sorcerers, weapons smugglers, U.S. Government assassins, and slingshot terrorists. No. She is *not* kidding. She even married one of them.

Sign up for her newsletter, get free books, and join the discussions on the forums when you visit her website at FJBlooding.com